Reality slammed over Juliana like an avalanche.

The plea for her baby's well-being that had been forming on her lips died the moment she saw the silent warrior in charge of the military compound where she was being held.

"Griffon?" she whispered. But she didn't need an answer. She knew the man before her.

He'd once given her the moon. And the stars. And a shining ray of hope.

Her heart ached at the sight of him. His shoulders were still as broad as she remembered, his body as lean and finely honed, his eyes still the color of the pines that dotted the Alps where they'd skied and laughed and loved together.

But he'd packed his bags and sneaked out in the middle of the night, leaving her alone...

...and pregnant.

Dear Reader,

April may bring showers, but it also brings in a fabulous new batch of books from Silhouette Special Edition! This month treat yourself to the beginning of a brand-new exciting royal continuity, CROWN AND GLORY. We get the regal ball rolling with Laurie Paige's delightful tale *The Princess Is Pregnant!* This romance is fair to bursting with passion and other temptations.

I'm pleased to offer *The Groom's Stand-In* by Gina Wilkins— a fascinating story that is sure to keep readers on the edge of their seats…and warm their hearts in the process. Peggy Webb is no stranger herself to heartwarming romance with the next installment of her miniseries THE WESTMORELAND DIARIES. In *Force of Nature,* a beautiful photojournalist encounters a primitive man in the wilderness and must find a way to tame his oh-so-wild heart.

In *The Man in Charge,* Judith Lyons gives us a tender reunion romance where an endangered chancellor's daughter finds herself being guarded by the man she's never been able to forget—a rugged mercenary who's about to learn he's the father of their child! And in Wendy Warren's new sensation *Dakota Bride,* readers will relish the theme of learning to love again, as a young widow dreams of love and marriage with a handsome stranger. In addition, you'll find an intriguing case of mistaken identity in Jane Toombs's *Trouble in Tourmaline,* where a world-weary lawyer takes a breather from his fast-paced life and finds his sights brightened by a lovely psychologist, who takes him for a gardener. You won't want to put this story down!

So kick back and enjoy the fantasy of falling in love, and be sure to return next month for another winning selection of emotionally satisfying and uplifting stories of love, life and family!

Best,

Karen Taylor Richman
Senior Editor

Please address questions and book requests to:
Silhouette Reader Service
U.S.: 3010 Walden Ave., P.O. Box 1325, Buffalo, NY 14269
Canadian: P.O. Box 609, Fort Erie, Ont. L2A 5X3

The Man in Charge

JUDITH LYONS

SPECIAL EDITION™

Published by Silhouette Books

America's Publisher of Contemporary Romance

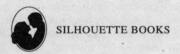 SILHOUETTE BOOKS

ISBN 0-373-24462-2

THE MAN IN CHARGE

Visit Silhouette at www.eHarlequin.com

Printed in U.S.A.

Books by Judith Lyons

Silhouette Special Edition

Awakened by His Kiss #1296
Lt. Kent: Lone Wolf #1398
The Man in Charge #1462

JUDITH LYONS

lives in the deep woods in Wisconsin, where anyone who is familiar with the area will tell you one simply cannot survive the bitter winters without a comfortable chair, a cozy fireplace and a stack of good reading. When she decided winters were too cold for training horses and perfect for writing what she loved to read most—romance novels—she put pen to paper and delved into the exciting world of words and phrases and, most important of all, love and romance. Judith loves to hear from her readers. You can contact her through her Web site, http:///www.judithlyons.com.

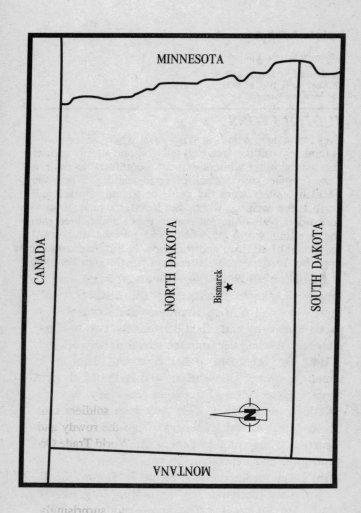

Chapter One

"I need to talk to the man in charge. Right now." Juliana Bondevik, daughter to the chancellor of Bjorli—a small oil-rich country in the North Sea—strode across the grass field between the two soldiers who had snatched her from the streets of her country.

Both the behemoth at her right and the Native American on her left were dressed in the black uniforms of her country's police, but they weren't Bjorlian officers. They were American soldiers sent by her father to whisk her away from the rowdy and sometimes rough protests against the World Trade Organization and deposit her here in America out of harm's way for the duration of the WTO convention.

"I'm sure the major will be waiting to greet you inside, Ms. Bondevik." The answer, not surprisingly, had come from the behemoth.

The other soldier, with his long, straight black hair, hadn't spoken a single word since he'd helped take her from the street in Bjorli. He just went about his business with a silent tongue and a maddening smile as if he were privy to some private joke.

But with any luck she wouldn't have to deal with her captors' idiosyncrasies beyond the next few minutes. If the major was waiting for her, surely she could convince him to send her back to Bjorli immediately. Surely he would understand she had to take care of her child.

A fresh surge of anger bubbled through her veins. She and her father were going to have a serious talk when she got back. He had no right to have her abducted off the street like some unruly teenager just because he was worried she'd get hurt in the protests. She could make her own decisions. She was a grown woman.

A mother, for pity's sake.

A fact that had obviously escaped her father's mind in his haste to have her spirited away to safety. But it was uppermost in her mind. At twelve months old, her daughter needed her. And she needed Perry. It had been twelve hours since she'd been abducted, and she already missed her daughter terribly. There was no way she intended to spend the next two weeks away from her just to appease her father's patriarchal worries. And whoever was in charge of this post *had better* understand her need to return home, on the double.

Speaking of this post, where *had* her father sent her? She took her first real glance around since stepping off the plane moments before. And came to a staggering halt.

With the military precision of her abduction and the noisy, uncomfortable plane she'd been whisked here in, she'd expected to find herself in a military installation. And much of what she saw fitted that picture perfectly.

Certainly this large valley had been chosen for its secluded, secure location. And the tall, chain-link fence topped with razor wire surrounding the two buildings and runway looked like any military installation she'd ever been in.

But the building in front of her made her think she'd landed in Oz. Or some other equally strange spot. She blinked. And then blinked again. But the building didn't change. She shook her head in amazed disbelief and looked up at the behemoth who'd stopped beside her. "A mansion in the middle of a military installation?"

He shot her an easy smile. "Well, it was here before the installation. Built in the Gilded Age, they tell me, very early nineteen hundreds when the timber barons and steamship and railroad owners were raking in their fortunes hand over fist."

She shook her head again, marveling at the odd combination. G.I. Joe meets the Vanderbilts.

The behemoth waved a hand toward the mansion, snapping her to attention. "The major is waiting for you, Ms. Bondevik."

She pushed aside the questions pinging in her head about what such a building was doing in the middle of a military installation and concentrated on what was important. Convincing the major to send her home to her child. With or without her father's consent.

They quickly strode over the remainder of the field to the mansion and climbed the staircase leading to a wide, stone veranda that ran the entire length of the building's facade. Crossing the veranda, she stepped through the door the silent warrior held open for her, a plea for her baby's well-being forming on her lips.

A plea that died the moment she saw the man waiting for them in the palatial foyer.

She stopped dead in her tracks, her blood crashing to her toes. "Griffon?" A bare whisper in the huge entrance hall with its beige marble floor and towering wooden pillars. But she didn't need an answer. She knew the man before her.

He'd once given her the moon. And the stars. And a shining ray of hope.

She stared, her heart aching at the sight of him. In his camouflage pants and tight, black T-shirt it was easy to see his shoulders were still as broad and proud as she remembered. His body as lean and finely honed. He still wore his sun-streaked blond hair a little long and shaggy. And his eyes...his eyes were still the color of the pines that had dotted the hills around the Swiss lodge where they'd skied together and laughed together and loved together.

Until she'd suggested they extend their relationship beyond their short vacation. Then he'd packed his bags and sneaked out in the middle of the night, leaving her alone...

And quite pregnant.

Pain washed through her, as sharp and painful as the morning she'd discovered he'd left. Lord, she'd been such a fool. She'd thought she'd found the real thing with Griffon Tyner. But all she'd found was a man looking for a good time. But...something good had come out of that pain. Something wonderful. Her daughter.

Perry.

Reality slammed over her like an icy avalanche. She stared at Griffon, fear sliding up her spine. Her abduction had nothing to do with the WTO protests. It was about her father's belief in parental rights.

She'd never told Griffon he was a father. A decision she and her own father had fought over endlessly. Her father believed Griffon had a right to know he had a daughter in this world. And because she'd never explained *why* she didn't want Griffon in her daughter's life, her father had taken matters into his own hands to make sure Griffon did know.

Panic racing through her, Juliana pulled her reeling emotions back together. She had to get out of this mess before Perry's future was put in jeopardy. She focused on Griffon. He looked as stunned to see her standing in front of him as she was to see him. Thank the Lord. If he was surprised to see her, it meant her father hadn't told him about his daughter. He was obviously giving her a chance to tell Griffon herself.

Not bloody likely.

Apparently recovering from his own shock, Griffon rocked back on his heels and cocked his brow in uneasy surprise. "*You're* the chancellor's daughter?"

She gathered her frantic emotions. If she was going

to get herself and her baby out of this mess, she needed a strong front. Squaring her shoulders, she lifted her chin and looked down her nose at him. "Poor Griffon. Does the phrase 'Hell hath no fury like a woman scorned' suddenly ring ominously in your head?"

He looked to his two henchmen—both of whom appeared more than a little interested in their conversation—and tipped his head toward the side of the foyer. "Privacy, gentlemen."

Her abductors moved to one end of a wide, beautifully designed staircase. Leaning against one of the ornately carved end posts, they waited for their next order.

She turned back to Griffon. "We don't need privacy. As much satisfaction as I might get out of telling you what a low-bellied, cowardly snake you are, I have more important things to do. Give me a phone. I'll call my father and put an end to this nonsense. And then you can put me back on your plane and have your soldiers fly me back to Bjorli." Her heart pounded in her chest. Please, let it be that easy.

But he just looked at her, his lips, lips that had once tantalized her in the dark of night, pressed into a thin, unhappy line. Finally he lifted a hand in supplication. "Listen—"

"I made the mistake of listening to you once, Griffon. I won't make that mistake again. The only thing I want to hear from you now is that you're putting me back on that plane and sending me home."

He looked away from her, a muscle along his jaw flexing. Finally he looked back. "I'll make the call and have it patched through to your room, Juliana. But don't get your hopes up. Your father made it clear he wants you safe and sound until the protests are over.''

Someone less acquainted with the man might think he looked guilty, sorry even. But Juliana knew better. ''Just get me the phone. I want out of here. Now.'' She gave him her best I'm-the-chancellor's-daughter-and-I-don't-want-any-argument look and prayed he wouldn't see through it to the desperation beneath.

The muscle in his jaw flexed again. ''I'll make the call, but I'm warning you right now, your father called on the king of Bjorli and Uncle Sam to help with these arrangements. So, at this stage of the game, it's going to take more than a call from your father to get you out.''

The world tilted beneath her feet. ''The king? And Uncle Sam? As in the president of the United States?'' She couldn't keep the alarm out of her voice.

He gave his head a single, succinct nod.

She should have seen it coming. There was no way her father could have had her abducted and not pulled the king into the plan. The Bjorlian guard protected the chancellor's family just as they protected the royal family.

Which is why the king had to have been involved. Juliana's guards had followed her to the protests. If the king hadn't been in on the kidnapping—and pulled her guards into the scheme—they would have risked their lives trying to protect her. On the long flight over here, she'd been relieved they hadn't been hurt in the scuffle, but now she realized they'd been in on the little plot all along. Wait until she saw them again.

As for the president of the United States, he would have been pulled in when her father informed the king he thought Griffon Tyner, a major in the U.S. Army, was the perfect person to pull off her kidnapping and keep her safe over the next few weeks.

Of course, none of this was about keeping her safe. Her father had only been interested in getting her stashed away somewhere private with Griffon where she could tell him of his daughter. A goal the king would have been sympathetic with, but never would have sanctioned. However, if her father had convinced the king she was in mortal danger at the protests, the king would have been happy to go along with her father's suggestions.

Lord. How was she going to extricate herself from this political mess? Well, she'd have to find a way. She wasn't letting Griffon into her daughter's life. No way.

She tipped her chin up. "Just lead me to my room, Griffon. And put that call through." Surely once she spoke to her father and told him what kind of man Griffon Tyner was, he'd make whatever calls were necessary to unravel this ugly web. And then he'd have her sent home immediately.

Surely he would.

Griff watched Matt Rutger and Talon Redhorse lead Juliana up the wide staircase, his heart pounding in his chest, a cold sweat covering his skin.

Juliana.

With her blue, blue eyes and velvety skin and sweet, curvy little body. Walking away from her had been the hardest thing he'd ever done.

And the most necessary.

It hadn't mattered that when she'd smiled at him, he'd felt like a conquering hero. Or that when her lips touched his, the darkness of his world had disappeared. Continuing to see her after his short stay at the lodge had not been an option. So he'd left, before the temptation to continue their relationship as she'd suggested had become too powerful to ignore.

But now she was here. In his house. With her tight stonewashed jeans reminding him just how sweet the soft curve of her hip was, and her T-shirt with its anti-WTO slogan emblazoned across her breasts reminding him just how full and sumptuous her upper curves were. And the pain and anger in her eyes telling him just how much he'd hurt her.

What a mess.

His midnight exit had been a coward's retreat. But leaving had taken all the courage he could muster at the time. Answering her questions about why he was leaving hadn't been doable. And it wasn't any more doable today.

He clenched his fists as Matt and Talon escorted her into the upstairs hall and she disappeared from sight. He'd give anything to be able to send her home, make her happy. But that wasn't doable, either.

Originally the little island of Bjorli had welcomed American troops as part of NATO's presence. But five years ago when oil was discovered in local waters, the U.S.'s mission in Bjorli had changed. Now the American troops helped guard the oil fields in exchange for much of the oil being shipped to the good old U.S. of A. In a time of uncertain oil flow from the middle east, Bjorli was a country the United States wanted to keep happy.

Which meant keeping the king of Bjorli happy.

So when the king had asked the president to arrange to keep the chancellor's daughter safe during the WTO convention, the president had been quick to oblige. And to handle the possibly sticky situation, the president had called on Griff.

And because 98 percent of Griff's business came directly from Uncle Sam, he too, had quickly obliged. And one simply did not change his answer to the president of the United States.

So Griff's only hope of sending Juliana home was her phone call to her father. If she could talk the chancellor into bringing her home, she could save not only herself, but Griff as well.

Because having her in his house where he could see her and smell her and want her, knowing he couldn't so much as touch her would kill him as surely as a sniper's bullet.

He turned on his heel and strode toward his office, employing a practice he hadn't used since he'd said good-bye to his mother at her funeral twenty-five years ago.

He prayed.

Please God, or whoever is supposed to be in charge of this mess down here, let her father send her home.

Chapter Two

Juliana set the phone back in its cradle with a shaky hand. According to Edward, her father's personal aide, the chancellor was "officially in a meeting until further notice." Her father would, however, find the time to speak to Griffon Tyner if the man had something *important* to say.

Juliana ran her hands down her jeans. She'd gotten her father's message loud and clear. He wasn't speaking to her until Griffon called to say he'd been apprized of his fatherhood.

She drew in a deep breath, trying to keep her thoughts calm. Her father might think he was doing the right thing by throwing her and Griffon together. But he was making a huge mistake.

She silently cursed her stubborn pride. She'd been too embarrassed to tell her father she'd fallen for a man's seduction. Too humiliated to tell him how Griffon had used her at the lodge for his own prurient pleasure and then tossed her away without so much as a by-your-leave. So her father didn't know Griffon Tyner was a user, didn't know she was afraid if she let Griffon into his daughter's life, he would use Perry for the money and status she could bring him without caring a whit for her tiny little heart.

If Juliana had only told him what kind of man Griffon was, this would never have happened. But she hadn't. And now Perry's future happiness was in serious danger.

Pain squeezed Juliana's heart. All her life, people had flocked around her, not because they liked her or because they felt any real kinship for her, but because being close to her provided access to her father and a certain social status.

Knowing that her "friends" were much more interested in what she could do for them than they were in Juliana herself was a painful reality she'd dealt with all her life. But knowing her daughter would someday face the truth that her *father* was hanging around simply for the advantages Perry could give him, was too painful to even contemplate.

Somehow Juliana had to keep that from happening. But how? She'd wanted to holler over the phone to Edward that if her father knew what kind of man Griffon Tyner was he wouldn't want him anywhere near his granddaughter. But any such revelation hadn't been possible.

The phone she'd just hung up wasn't an ordinary phone. It had no dialing mechanism on it. Any calls to or from this room had to be originated by someone else in the mansion. To think no one was monitoring her words would be a big mistake. It had been impossible to mention Perry at all. Impossible for her to say enough to convince Edward to bring her father to the phone.

Frustration scrambling up her spine, she looked around her room. Soft golds and pale blues shimmered in heavy satins and luxurious velvets as they hung from the tall windows and draped over the elaborately carved surfaces of the heavy furniture. But for all its opulent glory this room was nothing more than a prison cell. And if the telephone system hadn't been enough of a clue for her, the behemoth, who was even now standing guard outside her door, certainly was.

She began to pace, her nerves jangling under her skin, the rising panic stealing the breath from her lungs. How was she going to get out of this mess? Climb out the window? Sneak out of the compound and run to the nearest public phone or airport? It sounded like a bad action movie. But it might be her only choice.

She strode across the room to one of the many windows lining the outside wall and peered out. No bars, but then she obviously wasn't leaving the mansion this way. Her room was on the third floor, a good forty feet from the ground. And the wide stone veranda running in front of the mansion didn't invite any experimental jumping.

She turned back to her room. There had to be another way out of this mess. A knock on the door startled her out of her thoughts.

The behemoth? Or Griffon? She hoped for the behemoth. She wasn't ready to face Griffon again. The behemoth was more likely to answer her questions. And she had a ton of questions she needed answered if she was going to get out of this place. The first one being who Griffon's superior was. It seemed as if Griffon was in charge of this installation, but he had to have a boss somewhere. There was always a chain of command in the military. And if she could find out who the next link was, maybe she could convince that man to intercede on her behalf.

Taking a deep, fortifying breath, she pushed off from the windowsill, strode across the room and pulled the door open.

Griff stood in the doorway, staring at Juliana.

He'd been a fool to come up here. He should spend the next two weeks as far from this room and Juliana as his compound would allow. Teasing himself with her presence, knowing he could never have her, never so much as touch her, was a hair shirt he'd be a damned sight happier without. But he had come up here, anyway, telling himself he needed to make sure she was comfortable.

The biggest line of bull he'd ever employed.

The accommodations here were every bit as plush as she had at home. And Matt was posted outside her door, not only to keep her from disappearing, but to make sure she had everything she needed. Griff's presence here was absolutely superfluous.

But he had to see her again. Just see her. And now that he had, he should turn around and leave. But he wasn't going to do that, either. He couldn't. Not yet. The need to be in her company, if only for a moment, was far too strong. Sending Matt to stand guard farther down the hall, he brushed past Juliana into her room, drinking in her heat as he slid past.

Turning to her, he took in her expression. Anger and apprehension pulled at her brow. Definitely not emotions that would indicate she was going home. ''From your less-than-happy expression I take it your call to Daddy wasn't successful.''

She lifted a brow. ''From my expression? With your phone system here, am I supposed to believe you weren't listening in?''

She had every reason to think the worst of him for the way he'd sneaked out on her at the lodge. But still, the implication scratched at his pride. ''I don't eavesdrop on private conversations. Any call you make from this room will be between yourself and whoever is on the other end of the line. Period.''

She gave a humorless laugh. ''Oh, please, am I supposed to believe that while you feel no compunction about running out on a woman in the middle of the night, listening in on phone conversations is below you?''

It stung that she thought so little of him. Stung more that her anger was driven by pain. Pain he'd caused. And he didn't have to look very hard to see that pain. It was in the tight corners of her mouth, the protective way she held her body and the shadows clouding those blue, blue eyes.

But it was far less pain than he would have caused if he'd let their relationship go on, if he'd pulled her into the dark violence of his life. So he made no attempt to change her opinion of him.

She spun away from him, pacing around the room like a caged tigress. Those long legs eating the ground beneath them, the glide of muscle and bone as fluid and sensuous as any cat's.

He looked away trying to ignore the heat racing through him. Trying not to remember what it felt like to have those long legs wrapped around him. Encouraging him. Pulling him deep.

Finally she turned back to him, squaring her shoulders and leveling her blue-eyed gaze on him. "I want to talk to your superior."

He raised a brow. "My superior?"

"Yes. I know you're in charge of this installation, but you still have to report to someone. I want to talk to that officer."

Officer. He winced. She thought she was in a military installation. Not an illogical conclusion on her part. But finding out she didn't have someone higher up on the food chain to complain to wasn't going to make her happy. "I hate to tell you this, but I'm not part of the army anymore."

Her eyes snapped to thoughtful blue bands. "But they call you major."

"My old military rank. But this isn't a military installation. It's my compound."

"Your compound?" Disbelief colored her tone.

"Yes."

Her expression became intense, as if she were trying to fit the pieces of a particularly difficult puzzle together. "Not a government installation?"

"No. It's mine." He didn't even try to keep the satisfaction from his voice. He'd worked hard for this place. Sweated and fought and lost more than a few buckets of blood for it. And while he'd begun to realize over the last few years that his father's legacy was going to drag him down to the depths of despair and torment the old man had always planned for him, this house represented one battle Griff had won.

Her brow furrowed a little lower. "So the two thugs who abducted me aren't American soldiers?"

"No. They're my soldiers."

Confusion crossed her face again for one brief moment, but then her eyes popped wide as realization dawned. She took a protective step back. "Oh, Lord, you run a mercenary band." Disgust twisted her lips.

His stomach knotted at her revulsion. But he wouldn't deny the truth. Despite what sordid tales the word *mercenary* obviously conjured in her mind, he had nothing to be ashamed of. At least not on that front. He gave his head a succinct nod. "Yes. I run a mercenary band."

"No wonder you wouldn't tell me what you did for a living."

He hadn't told her for a million reasons, but none of them had to do with the scorn on her face now. "I'm not ashamed of being a mercenary. My men save people. People who would otherwise be forsaken because they're on the wrong side of a political argument. That's all that matters to me."

"Yeah, right. That and the tidy little sum that ends up in your bank account afterward." She looked away, shaking her head in disdain. But then she looked back at him, a sudden light springing into her eyes. "How much? How much would it cost for you to let me go?"

Another stinging blow. But this one he had to put straight. He met her blue gaze squarely. "Sorry, Jules. I'm not for sale."

Her brows snapped angrily together. "*Don't* call me Jules. I'm Ms. Bondevik to you. And what do you mean you're not for sale? You're a mercenary, aren't you? Your sword to the highest bidder and all that. I just need to know how high to bid."

He smiled sadly. Her contempt and anger were a poor replacement for the love and tenderness he'd once seen on her face. "Forget it, Ms. Bondevik. You're here for the duration. Adjust."

She huffed in frustration and strode away from him, her long stride gliding over the powder-blue carpet beneath her feet. When she turned back, a hint of panic furrowed her brow. "Am I a prisoner in this room then?"

He squashed the pang of guilt her obvious upset caused him. There wasn't anything he could do about her being stuck here. He was as much a pawn in this business as she was. She should have listened to her father when he asked her not to attend the protests. But he didn't want her to be miserable while she was here. "No, as long as you have a guard when you leave the room, you're free to wander at will."

"A guard?" she all but whined.

"A guard, *Ms. Bondevik.*"

It was time for him to go. He'd already seen far more than was good for him. He'd seen that her eyes were as blue as he remembered. That her hair was as long and silky blond. That she still made him wish for a future that could never be. And that he'd hurt her far more than he'd ever intended when he'd left her in Switzerland without a word.

He took a step forward. Despite knowing it was the last thing he should do, he reached out and touched her arm, drinking in her heat, the silkiness of her skin. An apology hovered on his tongue, but he squelched it. His manner of leaving her in Switzerland had been bad, but the motive behind it was rock solid.

And it was still rock solid today.

An apology wouldn't change that. It would only make things messier. And he didn't see how that would benefit anyone. Right now Juliana knew how she felt about him. She hated him. And Griff wasn't sure that wasn't best for both of them.

He dropped his hand, ignoring the deep emptiness that filled him as quickly as the loss of her heat drained from his fingertips. But he ignored the hollowness. It was something he'd grown used to.

He waved a hand toward the far corner. ''Your father sent your bags. He said everything you should need was in them. But if you're missing something, just let the man standing outside your door know. He'll make sure you have everything you need.''

He headed out of the room, his heart aching as hard as it had the first time he'd left her. There was no real need for him to cross her path again. His presence was only making her unhappy. And Matt and Talon would take care of her.

* * *

Juliana watched Griffon pull the door closed behind him, her arm tingling where he'd touched her, buzzing with the elemental recognition of a lover's caress. She rubbed the spot, trying to make the feeling stop. Trying to make the memories stop. Memories that gathered like doves in the morning dawn. Memories of dark nights, heated touches and soft, gentle laughter.

She closed her eyes, ruthlessly pushing the thoughts away. The memories weren't real. The days and nights she'd spent with Griffon Tyner had all been lies. Every word he'd whispered to her, every heated look, every ardent touch had been nothing more than a well-rehearsed seduction. A seduction he'd no doubt used on hundreds of women before her—and hundreds of women since.

She rubbed her arm harder. She had to get out of here. She stared at her closed door. She could hear the behemoth's heavy footsteps returning to his post. No exit there.

She stalked over to the window and peered out. It was every bit as far as she thought. Jumping was definitely out. And even if she tied all her bed linens together they wouldn't be long enough to get her to the ground safely. Too bad. Waiting until nightfall and sneaking out on Griffon in the middle of the night had a certain poetic justice to it. But unless someone stopped by with a forty-foot rope, it wasn't going to happen.

There had to be another way out. She racked her brain for possibilities. Griffon had said she was free to explore the compound—if a guard was with her. If she took a walk, incapacitated her guard, she could make a break for it.

She stared at the view outside her window. What she saw wasn't very encouraging. Only one guard tower kept watch over the entire valley. But with the stark barrenness of the landscape, one was probably enough. Very few trees and bushes had been allowed to grow between the mansion and low-lying hills that marked the edge of the valley. Making it to those hills without the guards spotting her would be tricky.

But if she planned the escape for the dim hours of dawn or dusk, stayed low and used what cover was available, she just might make it. She turned back to her room, her gaze settling on the luggage her father had sent. She could put on several layers of clothes to act as protection against the razor wire that topped the fence as she climbed over.

Hope wound through her veins. It might work. *If* she could incapacitate her guard. She ran her gaze over the room. There were plenty of small tables. She could pull a leg off one, hide it in her clothes and at the right moment kosh him over the head with it. Knock him out. Then she could scale the fence and head for the hills.

Of course, it would take quite a hit to knock out someone as big as the behemoth. She imagined the crunch of bone and flesh as she brought the table leg down on his head.

Oh, geez, the table leg was out. She just couldn't do that kind of violence to another human being. She continued studying the room. The curtain cords caught her eye, but she quickly dismissed them as

well. Strangling her guard was out, too. Her gaze
snagged on the four-poster bed with all its fancy,
carved knobs.

Fancy, carved knobs.

Yes.

She'd visited Argentina once with her father and
become intrigued by the bolo. A tool of the local cowboys. It consisted of two balls the size of small or-
anges each one tied to the end of a three-foot cord.

The first time she'd seen a cowboy swinging one
over his head as he'd galloped after a full-size bull,
the balls rotating in the air like helicopter blades, the
bolo had seemed more like a toy than a serious piece
of equipment. But when the gaucho had let go of the
cord and sent the bolo flying at the racing bull's feet,
she'd been amazed at how effective the simple tool
was.

The weight of the spinning balls had wrapped the
tough cord around three of the bull's legs, sending the
powerful animal crashing to the ground where he
could do nothing but wait for the cowboy's attention.

She'd been so intrigued with the bolo's efficiency
she'd looked up one of the cowboys after the dem-
onstration and had him show her how to use it. And
she'd practiced with the one he'd given her until
she'd become quite proficient with it.

With a bolo she could take someone as big as the
behemoth down without hurting him. And although
she wouldn't have much time to get over the fence
and sprint for the hills before he untangled himself,
sounded the alarm and came after her, it might just
work.

Yes it might.

Chapter Three

Dawn was just breaking as Juliana followed the behemoth down the stairs. Apparently, the giant soldier and his silent counterpart had been chosen not only as her abductors but as her personal guards, as well. The behemoth had taken the first round of guard duty yesterday evening when she'd arrived. The silent warrior had been leaning against the wall opposite her door when she'd made a trip to the bathroom during the night. And this morning the behemoth had returned.

And she was glad for his return. Long and lean, the silent warrior looked like a runner. She'd bet he was twice as fast on his feet as the behemoth. And since running was an important part of this escape, having the behemoth at her side had certain advantages. Not to mention that a long walk with the silent warrior held little appeal. Although, she had to admit the thought of tying him up and leaving him squirming while she made her getaway had a certain charm. Bet he'd make some noise then. But for this morning's endeavor she was definitely better off with the behemoth.

A few steps below her the giant soldier stepped off the stairs onto the beige marble floor of the foyer. "We'll go out the back way. I can pick up my jacket on the way out." He turned left and ducked into a small, narrow corridor tucked behind the stairs.

"I'm right behind you." Excitement surged through her, and she hopped lightly off the last stair, following the man into the narrow, dingy hall. With any luck the back of the compound would offer a better escape route than the front did.

She zipped her own jacket against the morning chill. She'd been greatly relieved this morning when she'd found the practical piece of clothing in the bags her father had sent. It had been about the *only* practical thing in the bag. Her father had obviously instructed her maid, Theresa, to pack with seduction in mind. The bag had overflowed with satins and silks designed to catch a man's eye.

The behemoth stopped at a small closet at the end of the hall, took out his jacket and struggled in the narrow space to pull it on.

She waited anxiously, trying desperately not to notice how big he was. How his shoulders practically spanned the cramped hallway. How the bulging muscles of his arms flexed as he settled the jacket into place. How strong—and lethal—his big hands looked as he worked his zipper.

A cold sweat coated her palms. She suddenly felt like David must have felt as he stood in Goliath's shadow loading his puny slingshot. Except her slingshot wasn't going to kill the mighty giant, only momentarily fell him. If she was lucky.

She nervously slid her hands into her jacket pockets, the fingers of her right hand caressing the homemade bolo. The drapery cord suddenly seemed as small and weak as a sewing thread as she looked at the behemoth's powerful legs. And the carved knobs seemed far too light to do their job.

She prayed he was as easy-going as he seemed. Because if there was a violent streak beneath his seemingly friendly nature and her trick didn't work and he caught her after she tried to knock him down, the morning could get ugly fast. Just thinking of those giant hands closing around her throat with all that raw power behind them sent chills down her spine.

But she couldn't think of that now. She had to get back to her daughter. She bounced restlessly on her feet. "Come on, oh mighty guard, let's go."

The behemoth smiled wryly, turned and opened the door behind him. "Why don't you call me Matt? Oh mighty guard is so...pretentious, don't you think?"

She chuckled softly, stepping past him and into the barest pink of early dawn. "Oh, I don't know, I think oh mighty guard has a certain appeal, don't—" The words died in her throat. "Oh, my Lord." The surprised whisper fell from her lips as she marveled at the backside of Griffon's compound.

When she'd first seen the mansion she'd thought it a single structure. But two full-size wings came off the back of the building, flanking a giant courtyard complete with an intricately laid brick surface, a spewing fountain, stone benches and a fair number of flowering garden beds.

She stared at her surroundings. "Well, this isn't exactly what I expected to find in a mercenary camp."

The behemoth raised a brow. "What? The extravagant architecture or the flowers?"

"Neither." She turned to the behemoth. "I don't suppose you'd like to tell me where this little outpost resides, would you?"

He shrugged. "I don't know why not. You're in North Dakota, Ms. Bondevik."

She shook her head. "*What* is a building like this doing in the middle of nowhere in North Dakota? And is Griffon's operation so big he needs all this space?"

"Griffon has about a hundred men, so we pretty much use the space." He nodded toward the front of the mansion where they'd just come from. "The company's offices are on the first floor, and the top two floors are Griffon's private residence." Now he nodded toward the east wing. "That wing is used for the barracks."

She spared only a quick glance at the barracks wing before turning toward the other wing. The west wing. Where rows and rows of big square windows had filled the other two wings, this one had long rectangular, stained-glass windows that ran from just under the roof to a foot or two above the ground. And a giant stone cross was mounted at the end of the roof. Obviously, whoever had built the place hadn't wanted to drive to town to worship.

She tipped her head toward the private church. "What do you use that wing for? Somehow I can't see you boys praying in it."

He raised a sardonic brow. "No?"

"Oh, come on. A horde of mercenaries? I don't think so."

"Ah, independent and unallied and therefore ungodly as well?"

She raised a brow. "You think that's an unfair perception?"

He shrugged those massive shoulders. "I don't know. As one of the unaligned my opinion is probably suspect. But from where I stand, it seems we're men like any others. We live, fight, pray, die."

She gave him a pointed look. "But what are you dying for? Honor and ideals? Or money and the thrill of bloodlust?"

A brief flash of sadness filled his eyes. A sadness so deep it startled her. But he quickly hid it with a congenial laugh. "All of the above. But not today. Come on, you said you wanted some exercise." He strode off, making it clear he was putting an end to the conversation.

She strode after him, wanting to ask about the sadness she'd seen in his eyes, but she squelched the impulse. She was about to dump him on his well-muscled posterior, something she had no qualms doing as long as she thought of him as her evil captor. But if she had to think of him as a human being with his own troubles, his own pains, she might have trouble throwing the bolo as hard as she needed to. And with Perry's happiness at stake she couldn't afford that.

Through the lightening rays of dawn, she scanned the new vista opening up as they hit the end of the courtyard. The perimeter fence waited for her halfway between the buildings and the hills, just as it had in front. But...

A small gathering of trees and bushes clustered in the middle of the back section of chain-link and coiled wire. Hope tickled her. The section of trees wasn't huge. It wasn't big enough to cover her escape until she hit the hills. But there was enough cover to allow her to bring the behemoth down and make her way over the fence without being seen.

She strode off the courtyard onto the mown grass, heading—as casually as she could manage—for the back fence. When the behemoth followed, obviously content to let her lead the way, she lengthened her stride and bee-lined for the trees. The sky was getting lighter by the minute. And she wanted this over with. Before she lost her nerve.

Quicker than expected, the little woods loomed before them. Excitement bubbled through her veins. The area of trees seemed much bigger up close than it had from the mansion. The success of her plan was looking better by the minute.

"Come on, oh mighty guard, let's go exploring." She ducked into the small forest, weaving around the bushes and trees, heading, she hoped, for the back fence.

She wanted the behemoth as far into the trees—and as close to the fence as possible—when she threw the bolo. The farther he had to run to get out of the forest to alert the guard, and the shorter distance she had to run to the fence, the better off she was going to be. And the forest wasn't so lush she worried about finding a space big enough to throw the bolo.

The behemoth followed her into the bank of trees as easily as he'd followed her out of the inner courtyard. And why not? With his superior size and strength, concern about her getting away was probably the last thing on his mind.

A crafty smile turned her lips as she moved deeper into the woods. Wasn't he in for a big surprise? Skirting another bank of bushes, she came to a stumbling halt. A small log cabin with a meandering stream curling by it sat in the middle of a tiny clearing.

Apprehension zinging through her, she turned to the behemoth. "You didn't say there was a cabin in here."

He stepped up next to her with an easy shrug. "You didn't ask."

If a soldier was in the little cabin her chances for escape had taken a serious dive. "Who lives here?" Panic edged her voice.

But thankfully the behemoth didn't seem to notice. He just shrugged those massive shoulders again. "No one. It's an old homestead. It's still here because Griffon can't bring himself to tear it down. Says if the place was tough enough to make it through the last 150 years it has a right to its little place by the stream."

She was quite certain Griffon wasn't capable of such a gracious sentiment. But she was greatly relieved to hear that the place was abandoned.

Relieved and fascinated. A pioneer's cabin.

While Juliana's father had come from a long line of Bjorlians, her mother had been American. And determined that Juliana would be as American as she was Bjorlian, her mother had been meticulous about Juliana's upbringing. Juliana had spent every summer at her grandparents' home in Kansas, half her college life in American universities and countless hours as a youngster listening to the American stories her mother read to her.

Juliana's favorites had always been the stories about the first American settlers. Stories like *The Yearling* and *Little House on the Prairie*. Stories about love and family and a simple way of life.

Now those stories seemed even closer to her heart. Because after struggling through one disastrous engagement—and a heartbreaking vacation at a little skiing village in the Alps—she knew that the simple, unencumbered love the men and women shared in those stories was out of the chancellor's daughter's reach.

Her curiosity piqued, she wandered closer to the cabin, taking in the split-log porch, the wavy glass of the antique windows and the giant logs, turned black by time, that made up the walls. "Do you know anything about the people who built it?"

The behemoth followed her to the cabin. "As a matter of fact, I do. According to local records this land was squatted by one Jedediah Crawford and his wife Liddy. They built the cabin together, supposedly finishing it just in time for their first child to be born in it.''

Smiling at the story, she stepped onto the old porch. A small heart-shaped window had been carved into the front door. A bit of whimsical frippery created by a husband to please his wife. She ran her finger wistfully over the sharp edge of the heart. A mother, a father, a tiny house, a tinier child...

And love.

Her heart squeezed. The Crawfords had been a lucky, lucky couple.

But she was lucky, too. She had a beautiful little girl with a loving smile and a sweet, innocent heart. A heart she needed to protect. And mooning away at this cabin, wishing for things that could never be, wouldn't get it done.

She pushed away from the door, leaped off the porch and jogged toward the winding stream running by the cabin. The fence, she was sure, was on the other side of the water. "Come on, oh mighty guard, we have more exploring to do.''

The behemoth sprinted after her. "Hey, why are we running all of a sudden?''

"I need the exercise.''

The behemoth made a sound of displeasure, but he didn't try to slow her down. He easily matched her pace.

As she got closer to the water, it became obvious the stream was nothing more than a shallow bubbling brook. Without breaking her pace, she jogged through.

She caught a glimpse of the chain-link through the trees up ahead. Exhilaration surged through her. She picked up her pace, dodging under trees and around bushes until she came to a small clearing running the length of the fence.

The behemoth slowed to a halt beside her. "End of the line, Ms. Bondevik. Now what?"

What indeed? The nervousness she'd felt in the hall returned tenfold. The moment was upon her. And the behemoth hadn't gotten one inch smaller, one ounce weaker.

She ruthlessly pushed those thoughts away and shoved her hand in her pocket. Ignoring the fact her fingers were sweaty and a little unsteady, she closed them over the spot in the bolo's cord she'd specifically folded so she could find the center of the throwing rope. All she had to do now was get enough distance between herself and the behemoth to pull the bolo out, get it swinging and toss it.

Before the man tackled her.

She strode into an restless pace, making a big show of gulping air, as if the little run had completely done her in. "Let me catch my breath and then we'll head back."

She puffed. She panted. She paced. And the whole while she studiously put more and more distance between herself and the behemoth. Finally, when she had a good twenty feet between them, she stopped and bent over, pretending to draw in great gulping breaths of air.

"You're out of shape. You should get out of your palace more often." Obviously deciding she wasn't going anywhere for a while, the behemoth turned his back on her and surveyed the surrounding woods.

Now. While his back was turned.

She straightened, pulling the bolo from her pocket. Apprehension squeezed the breath from her lungs. If he looked back now, she was done for.

Adrenaline poured through her. She started to swing the bolo over her head. It sputtered at first, refusing to settle into its usual smooth rhythm as trepidation affected her swing. But her confidence built with each rotation and in seconds the bolo was whirling over her head like a helicopter blade, the rope and wooden knobs whistling through the air.

The odd sound caught the behemoth's attention. He spun back to her, his eyes going wide as he saw the bolo swinging over her head. His eyes snapping to narrow, deadly bands, he spat a sharp curse and charged.

She jumped back, fear crashing through her. But she didn't stop swinging. With a final mighty sweep, she sent the bolo flying.

It flew through the air, angling sharply toward the behemoth's ankles. And then there was a whoosh and a snap as the cord found its mark and wrapped tightly around his legs.

He crashed to the ground.

Her heart seemed to burst in her chest. She'd *done* it. She dashed for the fence. But she hadn't gone two steps when her pace faltered.

What if she'd hurt him? Cursing her inconvenient and probably unwanted concern, she turned back to the behemoth.

He was flat out on the ground, shaking his head, as if he'd been knocked out and was trying to re-orient himself.

She took a step forward. "Are you all right?"

His head swung toward her, his eyes snapping into focus. And then he exploded into action with a low, angry growl, his powerful arms propelling him across the ground as he crawled toward her at a frighteningly fast rate, his legs fighting to kick the bolo free.

She leaped back with a startled scream. He was just fine. But if he caught her, she had serious doubts about *her* safety. She raced to the fence, her heart pounding hard and fast, dire warnings to "Stop or else!" from the behemoth hammering in her ears.

She threw herself at the fence, her hands and feet grappling for purchase in the small holes provided by the chain-link, the thick wire biting into her fingers. But she didn't think about any of that as she scrambled upward. She thought only of Perry.

She hit the top of the fence. All she had to do now was get over the razor wire.

"*Don't* try to go over that wire," the behemoth hollered at her from the ground where he worked to free the bolo from his ankles. "*Get back down here, dammit.* That wire will snag you like a hare and cut you to pieces."

His warning plucked at her already-screaming nerves, but she forced herself to ignore him. He was going to be in big trouble if she got away. He'd prob-ably say anything to get her back down on his side of the fence.

Adrenaline pouring through her, she plunged one

arm through the tightly woven coils and grasped the top rail. Relief swept through her when she didn't feel the sharp bite of the wire. The extra clothing was working.

She plunged the other arm in, grabbed the top rail and held on as her toes clambered toward the top. But when she realized she needed a wider grip to keep her balance, and she tried to pull one arm free to move it, the springy wire wrapped around her arm. And grabbed hold like it had a life of its own.

She winced as the wire sliced through her layers of clothing and bit into her. Pushing her arm forward, she tried to get the wire to loosen its hold. But it only tightened more, sinking its razor teeth deeper into her flesh.

And then her feet started to slip.

Chapter Four

Sweat trickling into his eyes, Griff threw the next punch as hard as he could, connecting with the heavy sandbag with a painful thud. He'd been here in what used to be the church's sanctuary and was now his compound's gym since long before dawn. But the sun was up now, streaming through the tall, stained-glass windows, splashing colored patches of light across the red mats and stone floors.

His body was exhausted, spent. He ought to be able to sleep standing up. But he knew the minute he closed his eyes images of Juliana would flood his mind. Flood his mind and his body, making sleep impossible. He laughed roughly, humorlessly and threw another punch. Closed his eyes? Who was he kidding? He couldn't stop the images from flashing through his head with his eyes wide open.

Juliana skiing down a snow-covered mountain, her cheeks pink from cold and high spirits. Juliana sitting on one of the lodge's cushy sofas with a mug of hot cocoa, smiling and laughing as they told stories and jokes. Juliana lying in his bed, her smooth, silky skin gilded by the firelight, her sky-blue eyes smoldering with passion.

Damn.

He threw another bone-jarring punch and feinted away, his feet dancing through a patch of purple light as the bag swung back at him.

The door at the end of the sanctuary opened, the sound echoing in the cavernous room. A soldier's quick footsteps headed toward him. "We got trouble at the back fence, Major." Cash Ryan's voice carried across the long room.

Griff spun toward his chief of security, his senses kicking into full alert. He was keeping his promise to himself, staying away from Juliana. But he was keeping track of her. She'd headed out for a walk with Matt a half hour ago. And now there was a problem outside. "What kind of trouble?"

"Apparently, Ms. Bondevik decided she'd had enough of our hospitality. She knocked Matt down somehow and tried to climb the fence. They're cutting her out now."

Cutting her out. His gut clenching in a hard knot, he jerked off his boxing gloves and pitched them on a nearby bench. "Get Matt on the radio. *Now.*"

"Already done."

Of course it was done. Cash Ryan was always at the top of his game. Griff grabbed the radio Cash handed him, smashed the talk button and barked into the small, black box. "What the *hell* is going on out there?"

"Nothing now." Matt's voice crackled over the radio. "We're headed back to the church. Can you meet us at the infirmary with the doc?"

The doc. Griff's gut clenched harder, and the sweat covering his body turned cold. "How badly is she hurt?" He was already moving, his feet automatically carrying him to the side door that led to the infirmary.

"Not bad," Matt reassured. "She's moving under her own steam. But she got into the wire—"

He smashed the talk button again, cutting Matt off. "How the hell did she get clear to the top of the fence?"

An irritated sigh sounded on the other end of the radio. "It's a long story, sir."

"It better be a damned impressive story, or you're going to spend the next week practicing hand-to-hand combat with Talon." He handed the radio back to Cash who'd fallen in step beside him, their footsteps echoing in the high ceilings. "Get the doc to the infirmary."

"The doc's on his way. Do you want me to debrief Matt when he gets in?"

Griff pulled his lips into a feral smile. "Oh, no. *I'll* take care of Matt."

"Got it." Cash turned on his heel and headed back the way he'd come.

Griff yanked the side door open and strode into the small hall that housed the armory and infirmary. But he didn't head to the clinic. He needed to get to Juliana *now*. He crossed the hall and pushed out the door leading to the inner courtyard.

The crisp morning air chilled his sweaty skin, and the sound of the Jeep approaching from the back acreage sounded in his ears. The Jeep pulled onto the inner courtyard's bricks just as the door closed behind him. His gaze zeroed in on Juliana.

She was sitting in the back with Matt, her long hair tousled, her complexion pale. But she was sitting up, not lying down, and he couldn't see any injuries from here. No blood. Nor, despite her obvious upset, did she look to be in any real pain. The knot in his gut eased just a bit as the Jeep closed the distance and came to a stop beside him.

Griff jerked open the Jeep's door, his gaze quickly taking in the portion of Juliana the door had hidden from view. "You all right?"

"No," she snapped. "Your stupid fence just about cut my arms off."

The knot in his gut unwound. If she could snap at him like that, she was all right. A little cut up, but all right. He quickly surveyed her arms. The sleeves of her navy blue canvas jacket had several slashes in them, but there was very little blood. Amputation was a long way off. But the way her hands shook in her lap told him her encounter with the fence had left her shaken.

He reached in and gently took her arm. "Come on. The doctor's waiting. He can sew your limbs back on."

And once that was done, Griff was going to read her the riot act. What the hell had she been thinking, trying to climb over that fence? And how the hell had she gotten by Matt to do it?

He turned to the giant soldier. "Wake Talon and send him to the infirmary to pick up Juliana when the doc is done. Then wait for me in my office."

Matt vaulted out of the Jeep, his expression grim. "Got it." Without another word he headed across the courtyard.

If Matt had been lax in some way there would be serious consequences. But all that would come later. Right now, Griff had to take care of Juliana. He dismissed the men in the Jeep and tightened his hold on her elbow. "Come on, let's get you to the infirmary."

She tried to pull out of his grip. "I can walk on my own. I don't need your help. I don't *want* your help."

But he only tightened his hold. "Don't be stupid, you're shaking so hard you're about to fall down." And right now he needed to touch her. Needed the feel of her to assure himself she was all right.

He led her into the church, down the narrow hallway to the compound's clinic and settled her on the examination table. He didn't think he was going to find any major damage, but he wouldn't know for sure until he got her coat off.

He'd barely gotten the jacket unzipped when Mikey, the young intern he'd hired just out of medical school six months ago, pushed through the door, out of breath and primed for disaster. "What happened?"

Griff carefully pulled one sleeve free. "Ms. Bondevik attempted an unscheduled departure. Got caught in the razor wire."

Mikey nodded and reached for the second jacket sleeve, his youthful expression all business. "I can get it, sir."

Griff didn't want him to get it. *He* wanted to get it. *He* wanted to make sure she was okay. But Juliana was already holding her arm out to the young man. And she was shooting Griff a look that clearly said she would just as soon he dropped off the face of the earth.

So Griff backed off. But he didn't go far. Just to the other side of the room where he leaned against a supply cabinet and kept his eyes glued to Juliana.

Mikey finished pulling the tattered jacket off and set it aside. A soft, button-up, pale blue sweater that made her eyes shine like two aquamarine stones emerged. But it was the long slashes and red stains on the arms that caught Griff's attention. He gritted his teeth as Mikey pulled the torn material apart at the biggest, bloodiest tear and peeked in.

Lifting his head from the injury, he said something to Juliana. She answered him, but Griff didn't have any idea what they were saying. Their voices were too low to make out the words. But as soon as Juliana stopped talking, Mikey started unbuttoning the top of the sweater while Juliana's fingers worked up from the bottom.

Desire, white-hot and lightning quick, tore through Griff. He knew what it felt like to unbutton Juliana's sweaters. Knew the heat her skin gave off. Knew how the generous swell of her breasts pressed against a man's fingers. Knew how her nipples peaked when a man's knuckles brushed over them as buttons were undone.

And he damned well didn't want any other man feeling those things.

But the man unbuttoning her blouse wasn't a lover, he reminded himself, taking a tight hold on the green-eyed monster racing through him. Mikey was a doctor. His touch was purely clinical. And Juliana needed the attention. So Griff shoved his hands in his pockets and gritted his teeth while the kid did his work.

As soon as the buttons were undone, Mikey peeled the blue sweater off to reveal another shirt below. This one a stark white satin that accented the paleness of her cheeks and the seeping red splotches on her sleeves. A satin blouse, with rhinestone buttons. His brow pulled low in thought. What was wrong with this picture?

But before he could nail it down, Juliana and Mikey exchanged another volley of low words and their fingers went to work again, pulling the sparkling buttons from their holes. Before long the satin blouse was off and the smooth shimmer of peach silk appeared.

Another shirt.

Realization dawned, anger rushing through him. He narrowed his eyes on her. "*That* was your idea of protection against razor wire? Three layers of satin and silk?" He couldn't believe she would try something so foolish. That she would stupidly put herself in such danger for something so trivial as a few missed WTO protests.

Fire flashed in her eyes and she drew a breath for

a sharp retort. But her attention was diverted when Mikey clasped the bottom of her buttonless, silky peach blouse and started to pull it over her head. She grabbed his hands, pushing them back to her waist. "No. I'm not taking my shirt off. Not with *him* in here." She shot Griff a pointed glance.

Mikey dropped his hands from the blouse as if he'd been burned, color flushing his cheeks. "Sorry. I should have thought." He turned to Griff. "Do you want to wait outside?"

Griff shook his head. He wasn't going anywhere until he saw how much damage she'd done to herself. But he could understand where she might feel uncomfortable about being topless with two men in the room. With *him* in the room.

He looked back to her defiant gaze. "Are you cut anywhere besides your arms?"

She shot him a confused scowl. "What difference does that make?"

"Are you?"

"No."

He looked back to Mikey. "Just cut the sleeves off."

She hissed in exasperation. "Why don't you just leave?"

He looked back to her, his gaze direct, hard. "I'm not going anywhere until we have a little chat."

"I don't have anything to say to you," she spat.

He laughed humorlessly. "Don't worry, you won't have to utter a word." He crossed his arms over his chest, making it clear he wasn't going anywhere as

Mikey cut the sleeves from her blouse and pulled them from her arms.

Griff's gut clenched when he saw all the blood smeared over her arms. Maybe she'd been hurt worse than he thought. "How bad is it?" he asked, his voice tight, tense.

Mikey grabbed a handful of gauze pads from a nearby table, doused them in alcohol and started wiping up the blood. "I don't think it's as bad as it looks. But give me a minute to make sure."

Mikey worked quickly, efficiently as he wiped away the blood, uncovering the cuts and assessing the damage. But it wasn't quickly enough for Griff. "Well," he prodded, after a very short minute.

Mikey looked over his shoulder at him. "Nothing serious. A good cleaning and a few bandages, she'll be good as new."

Juliana gave them both a nasty scowl. "Would you two mind *not* talking about me like I'm not here."

Mikey's head whipped back to Juliana. "Sorry, ma'am—uh, Ms. Bondevik. Didn't mean to—"

Griff cut in before the man could grovel any further. "Don't let her fluster you, Doc. Now, back to her injuries. Cleaning and bandages? That's it?"

Mikey nodded.

Griff pushed away from the cabinet. "I'll take over then."

Mikey's brows snapped up in surprise. "You, sir?"

He shot the young puppy a sardonic look. "I've got my first aid badge, Mikey. You needn't worry I'll damage her."

The kid's cheeks colored again. "Sorry, sir. Didn't mean to imply—"

He shot the doctor a hard look and tipped his head toward the door. "Out, Mikey." He and Juliana had things to discuss. And if there was the added bonus that no one would be touching her but him—good.

Finally getting the message, Mikey nodded his head in salute and practically flew out of the room.

Juliana scowled at him. "Do you like to terrorize everyone?"

"I'm not terrorizing anyone. Yet."

"Oh does that mean you're going to terrorize me next? Am I supposed to be shaking in my boots?"

He wished she were shaking in her boots. It would make his job a hell of a lot easier. But her mutinous expression didn't hold an ounce of fear. Or good sense, either. He picked up one of the pads Mikey had soaked in alcohol and started swabbing at her arm. "What the hell were you thinking, trying to climb over that fence?"

"I was thinking you wouldn't let me out so I had to think of some other way to go home."

"For a few stupid protests?" He didn't even try to keep the anger out of his voice as he swabbed at one of the larger cuts.

She winced and jerked away as the alcohol seeped into the slash. "*Ouch.* No. To get away from you." She jerked again. But not from pain this time. From the words that had slipped from her mouth.

She hadn't meant to say them. He could see it in the stain flushing her cheeks. The upset from being caught in the fence egged on by the sting of alcohol had no doubt brought those words to her lips. But she'd meant them.

His hand hovered over the cut he'd been cleaning, the implication of those words sinking in. She hadn't climbed the fence because her father had kidnapped her and sent her to a safe house while her precious protests went on. She'd risked the viciousness of the razor wire to get away from him.

Damn.

Had he thought offering no apology had been best? God, he was an idiot. When would he stop making mistakes with this woman? When would he stop hurting her? It was true that leaving her in Switzerland had been his only option. Letting their relationship go on—no matter how sweet the temptation—would have been unconscionable. But had he really thought an apology for the way he'd left would make things any worse?

He stared at the cuts criss-crossing Juliana's arms. How could it possibly have been any worse?

He needed to fix this. Somehow. He tossed the bloody pad and grabbed a clean one, his hands not quite as steady as they'd been. "I'm sorry about Switzerland. I—"

"I don't want to hear it." She held her hand up, forestalling his words. "Whatever it is, I don't want to hear it. I was stupid enough to fall for your seduction, but I *won't*—"

"Seduction?" His brows snapped together.

"Oh, come on, you think I didn't figure out your poor-lonely-man routine? You think after you disappeared in the middle of the night I didn't realize all the wonderful words you'd whispered in my ear were just empty come-on lines you'd honed to perfection?'' She shook her head, as if she still couldn't believe her own gullibility. ''That if I hadn't fallen for your ruse the next woman would have? And you would have been just as happy with her.''

''Is that what you think? That any woman would have done?''

''Of course it's what I think. It's the truth.''

But it wasn't the truth. In fact, it was so far from the truth as to be laughable—if the reality of the matter wasn't so pathetic.

He wasn't a womanizer. Never had been. Never would be. Inviting a woman into his life was far too risky. For him. For her. For everyone involved. So he did his best to live a monk's life. A lonely, empty existence, but the only one the tainted blood running through his veins allowed. The only one his conscience could live with. And the only exception he'd ever made to that rule had been...Juliana.

And now she was paying for his one moment of weakness.

Not only with the blood oozing from her cuts, but with the pain he heard in her voice and saw in her eyes. He turned away from her, his hands shaking as he reached for a tube of antibacterial ointment. ''Any woman wouldn't have done.''

''Oh, please, you don't really expect me to believe that, do you?''

No. Not after the way he'd left her at the lodge. The only way he could convince her he was telling the truth was to give her the truth. His gut clenched. He couldn't do that. Not even to chase away her pain.

Another slash to his soul. Not that it mattered. His soul was so black, a few more marks weren't going to make any difference. Hell was waiting for him as surely as it had waited for his father before him. And there wasn't a damned thing Griff could do about it. The die had been cast long before he'd been born.

Ignoring the unsteadiness of his hands, he quickly spread ointment on her wounds and covered them with bandages. The sooner he handed her over to Talon, the better. She would be better off in anyone's hands but his.

Chapter Five

Juliana paced the thick blue carpet of her room. Since her failed escape attempt two days ago, the silent warrior had replaced the behemoth as her daytime guard. Now the behemoth guarded her door at night. His punishment, she guessed, for letting her get to the fence.

Unfortunately, the change of guards wasn't the only change in her routine. Griffon had revoked most of her privileges, as well. She was no longer allowed to wander either the grounds or the mansion at will.

Now, with the exception of bathroom trips, she was allowed out of her room only once a day to get a little exercise walking the mansion's halls, her route specifically chosen by her guard.

Obviously, Griffon wanted to make sure she couldn't snoop around for a fresh escape route. She grimaced. She hadn't seen Griffon since the day of her failed escape attempt. He'd bandaged her up, passed her off to the silent warrior and disappeared from her life. A circumstance that should have thrilled her. But it didn't.

Any woman wouldn't have done. The words rang in her head like an insistent song, messing with her head and pulling at her heart.

She wanted to believe them.

Wanted to believe the time they'd shared together at the lodge had been real. Wanted to believe that at some point in her life someone had cared for her, the person, not the chancellor's daughter. Just as she wanted to believe the heat his touch had brought while he'd cleaned her wounds in the infirmary yesterday was something she could thrill to instead of chiding herself for.

Foolish. And unutterably stupid.

He *hadn't* meant what he'd said in the infirmary any more than he'd meant the words he'd whispered in her ear at the lodge. He'd no doubt uttered them to make her think he cared, believing she'd be more pliable, less likely to try another escape. And believing anything else was more than stupid. For Perry, it was downright dangerous.

Juliana never wanted her daughter to experience the feeling of betrayal that had seared her the morning she'd discovered Griffon gone. Never.

With an angry growl she opened the French door that led to the balcony and strode out. Cold, damp air cloaked her, raising goose bumps on her skin and sending a chill down her spine. She had to find a way out of this bloody compound. Stepping over to the wrought-iron railing, she stared down to the long veranda below. It was still just as far down as it had been the other day. Blast.

Clenching her fists, she paced from one end of the balcony to the other. Even if she got out of this room, out of the mansion, what then? She'd already discovered she wasn't going over that fence. So what did that leave?

Wait a minute. What about under?

Excitement zipped along her veins. She obviously wasn't going to be tunneling under the thing, but she might be able to sneak under the wire where the stream ran under the fence. It might work. And if there wasn't quite enough room, she could dig a space big enough. The wet dirt would be soft, easy to move. And there wasn't enough water in the stream to make it a hazard. Maybe all she *did* have to do was get out of this room.

Ignoring the day's chill, she stared through her chamber to the door on the other side. No sneaking out that way with her guard waiting on the other side. And she'd already decided getting to the ground from here was futile. So if she wasn't going down or through...

She tipped her head back and stared at the drain gutters hanging about nine feet above her head. More excitement washed over her. She couldn't reach the roof from here. But if she stood on the balcony railing she'd be able to. And once she was on the roof she was bound to find a drain pipe she could shinny down. She'd been a master tree climber as a kid.

She smiled triumphantly. The dreary day was looking better by the minute. Now all she had to do was find something decent to wear. She glanced down at the silk robe she had on. She'd sent her jeans and T-shirt out to be washed an hour ago, and Talon had said she shouldn't expect them back before tomorrow.

She sighed. The robe was definitely not roof climbing apparel. And neither were the dresses filling her luggage. But if she dumped her bags out, surely she'd find something that would work. And then all she'd have to do was wait for the concealing cloak of night.

Griff sprawled in his big leather wing chair, his feet stretched out to the fire crackling in the fireplace and a full whisky glass cradled in his hand. He didn't normally have a fire in the middle of the summer, but it was cold this evening. The storm that had threatened all day had finally broken with a fury about twenty minutes ago. It was cold and wet, and the chill had sunk into his bones. So he'd started the fire in the study's giant fireplace and grabbed a bottle of whisky—and here he sat, listening to the rain pummel the mansion and the thunder shake the skies.

He took his first swig of JD, the fiery liquid burning a path to his gut. Not that he was drinking to warm up. Oh no. The whisky was to numb his brain. Make him forget, if only for a while, that Juliana was under his roof. Make him forget the anger and sadness he saw in her eyes when she looked at him. Make him forget just how soft her skin was.

He laughed humorlessly, the hollow sound echoing through his study like old ghosts. He could drink until the hounds of hell came after him, and he'd still remember the sadness he'd put in her eyes. And how soft her skin was. Soft and silky and, oh, so damned inviting.

He shook his head. He wished he was the big-time womanizer Juliana thought he was. Maybe he wouldn't be strung so tight if he'd slaked his need some time in the past six months. But he hadn't. He made a habit of stretching his needs to the breaking point. Then he released his tension with a woman who wanted exactly what he did. A quick tumble and a quicker goodbye.

It was never very rewarding, but it was the only safe thing to do. If a man spent his time gathering women into his life, sooner or later he found one he wanted to keep. Someone he wanted to start a family with. And family, hearth and home weren't for him. No matter how much he wanted them.

And he wanted them. Like a man dying of thirst wanted water, dreamed of water, prayed for water, he wanted a family to call his own. He dreamed of a woman's soft touch, prayed for the sound of a child's jubilant laughter. But his violent past would destroy them as surely as it had destroyed Griff, so he'd never risked the temptation of letting women into his life.

Until Juliana. Sweet, gentle Juliana. She'd caught him with his guard down.

He'd headed to the little lodge in Switzerland after returning home from a horrific campaign. A campaign where every day had meant facing the butchered bodies of not only men and soldiers, but boys just on the brink of manhood. Boys far too young to be carrying guns. When he'd finally gotten home, he'd been heartsick and…empty. So he'd fled to a place where he knew the halls and rooms would be full of people. People who were living and breathing and smiling and laughing and having fun.

But even the busy lodge hadn't dispelled the hollowness inside him. He'd pounded down the slopes with hundreds of skiers, eaten dinner in restaurants teeming with people and sat for hours on end in the lodge's great room, watching the flames in the giant fireplace and listening to the people around him boast about the day's runs. But the emptiness hadn't abated. If anything it had grown deeper and darker and colder.

And then Juliana had come along with her shy smile, an extra cup of hot cocoa and an invitation to share a few minutes with her. Every coherent cell in his body had told him to send her on her way. And he might have, if he hadn't looked into her eyes. But when he saw a loneliness as deep and aching as his own reflected back in Nordic blue, sending her on her way had been impossible.

From that moment on, everything had just snowballed. She'd been so beautiful and kind and full of joy. And so damned giving.

She'd been everything he'd ever dreamed of on every dark, lonely night of his life. And he'd taken everything she'd had to give. Taken it and devoured it and savored it like a dying man grabbing every bit of life he could find in his final hours. And now she was in his house. Making him remember how beautiful she was. How beautiful and soft and—

Two urgent raps shot through the study's brooding silence. "Major, we've got a situation on the roof." Cash's voice filtered through the thick study door.

Griff snapped out of his dark musings, alarm charging through him. "Come in." He thrust out of his chair, set his glass on the mantel and strode toward the door.

Cash pushed into the study, his expression tight. "Ms. Bondevik is on the roof. She's hanging on to one of the chimneys, trying not to get washed down by the weather."

"Oh, hell." The mansion's roof was steeply pitched. Even on dry, sunny days the roof tiles were slippery. In the rain they'd be treacherous. And Juliana was out there. In the dark. In this raging storm.

He strode by Cash into the hall, his heart pounding, fear ringing in his ears. "Did you send someone for the climbing gear? We'll need ropes."

Cash followed him out, stretching his stride to fall into step beside Griff. "Marshall's on his way. He'll meet us in Ms. Bondevik's room."

Griff kicked into a run, adrenaline pumping through his veins, his footsteps pounding on the marble floors and echoing in the high ceilings. They had to get her down. Fast.

Cash ran beside him as they sprinted for the stairs.

"How the hell did she get on the roof?" Griff asked as they hit the steps and bounded up.

"The only thing we can figure is that she climbed onto the balcony railing and climbed up from there. When Matt heard the scream he rushed in and found the French doors open, the rain blasting into the room.

When he went out onto the balcony he found Ms. Bondevik on the roof, clinging to the chimney.''

Cash gave his head a mad shake, his lips curled in self-disdain. ''I should have had a guard out there. But it never occurred to me she'd try to escape out the balcony. It's too high. And up?'' Disbelief sounded in his voice.

Griffon understood perfectly. It hadn't occurred to him, either. But Juliana had thought of it. Because she was desperate to get away from him. Dammit.

They hit the second floor, hammered up the next set of stairs and rushed to Juliana's room. When they got there, they found Marshall and Matt already on the balcony, the rain pouring down on them. A pile of climbing gear lay at Marshall's feet, and he clenched a rope with a high-tech grappling hook in his hands. Griff and Cash rushed out to join them, the cold rain drenching them as they stepped onto the small enclosure.

''How's she doing?'' Griff hollered as he squinted into the darkness, trying to see Juliana. But the night was too dark, the rain too heavy to see anything.

''She's hanging on,'' Matt hollered back. ''You'll see during the next lightning strike. You're gonna love it.''

Griff's gut twisted at Matt's dark warning, but he pushed the dread aside and turned to Marshall. ''You going to set that on the peak?''

Marshall gave him an answering nod. ''Trying. But the wind's giving me fits.''

''Try again.'' Griff turned to Matt. ''Go change

into something dry, then get back here to finish off your shift.''

Matt's lips pressed into an unhappy grimace. "I'm sorry. This is my fault.''

Griff shook his head, his own lips pressed into an unhappy line. "No one expected this. Just get changed and get back here.''

With a short nod Matt disappeared through the French doors.

A flash of lightning lit the sky, and Griff glanced up. The picture that met his gaze stopped him cold. The icy rain sluiced down the roof in waves. Halfway up the steep pitch and about ten feet over to the right of the balcony Juliana clung to one of the brick chimneys, her feet dangling toward the edge of the roof and the three story drop below.

His heart pounding a frenetic tattoo, Griff snatched up a climbing harness from the pile of equipment and strapped it on. He opened his mouth to tell Marshall to get the damned rope up, but the wind had momentarily abated, and the man was already taking advantage of the situation, swinging the line hard and giving it a mighty toss. This time it flew high, sailing over the roof's peak. With a hard, quick yank, Marshall set the hook.

Before his man could hook the thick, sodden rope to his own climbing harness, Griff took it from his hands. "I'm going up. You spot.''

With a quick nod, Marshall took the end of the rope as it fed out through Griffon's harness and took a wide stance, anchoring himself as ground position.

His fingers already clumsy from the icy rain, Griff

grasped the wet rope and pulled hard, balancing himself as he climbed onto the narrow wrought-iron railing. The driving rain obscured what little vision he had. He had to rely more on feel than sight to secure his footing as he climbed onto the roof. His feet slipped on the wet tiles, the rough rope biting into his hands as he struggled to keep his footing. God. And Juliana had been up here with no lifeline. A hard chill flashed down his spine, mixing with the icy rain.

"Juliana, can you hear me?" He hollered into the dark, stormy night. He needed to hear her voice. Needed to know she was still holding on. Still okay.

"I can hear you." Another flash of lightning lit the sky, and he could see her shifting her weight, looking over her shoulder toward him. Her face was pale in the brief light, her lips drawn into a thin tense line, her eyes filled with alarm.

"How ya doing?" he called into the resumed darkness, trying to calm her fears. At least for now. When he got her safely in her room he had every intention of reminding her just how scared she was. Just how much she'd scared *him*.

"I'm freezing." Her voice shook.

"Hang on. I'm almost there."

The roof tiles were as slick and treacherous as he feared, but he finally managed to slip and slide his way over to her. Holding on to the rope with one hand, he leaned over and wrapped his free arm around her middle. "Gotcha. Now, don't let go of the chimney. Use your grip to help yourself to your feet. Then I'll get you snuggled in front of me and we'll head down. Okay?"

"Got it." She scrambled to her feet.

It wasn't easy, but with his support and help he soon had her standing in front of him, her back snuggled into his front. "Grab hold of the rope."

Lightning flashed again, illuminating their surroundings as she grabbed the rope, wrapped her hands tightly around it and snuggled back into him, securing her position.

Bracketing her with his arms, he let go and took hold of the rope with both hands. "Okay, we're going to head over to the balcony with little steps. The roof is too slippery to support big ones. And then we'll lower back down to the balcony. Got it?"

She nodded and they started the slow, slippery trek. The rain was icy cold as it pelted them, but where their bodies were snuggled up tight against each other the heat started to build. The last thing he needed to be thinking about was how good her cute little butt felt snuggled against his lap. Or remembering how perfectly that lovely bottom had fit in the curve of his palm. But he couldn't keep the erotic thoughts from rampaging through his mind.

How many nights had he lain awake thinking of a woman's softness? Juliana's softness. And now she was nestled up tight against him from collarbone to knee. Man.

Trying desperately to switch his mind from his suddenly pounding libido, he concentrated on the task at hand as they moved carefully across the roof. And, thankfully, before long they were directly over the balcony. With Cash's and Marshall's help he lowered himself and Juliana safely from the roof.

He stepped away from Juliana's tempting body as soon as their feet hit the balcony's floor. The icy cold rain doused his front, cooling his ardor and his flesh. Taking hold of Juliana's shoulders, he turned her toward the French doors. "Go in and grab a blanket before you freeze to death."

She turned back to him, her tension drawing the lines of her face tight. "I suppose I should thank you."

Now that she was safely on the ground, her fear had gone, leaving only her frustration at her failed escape attempt behind. Too bad. He gave her a hard look. "I suppose you should."

Her lips compressed a little more as she shivered against the cold. "Thank you."

"You're welcome. Now go inside and get yourself wrapped up."

"You don't have to tell me what to do. I'm quite capable of taking care of myself." She turned away from him and started into her room.

Yeah. The last ten minutes had convinced him of that. He leaned inside after her. "Don't even *think* about stepping out of this room."

"Where would I go?" she mumbled, crossing the room toward her bed as she rubbed some warmth into her arms.

He shuddered to think what escape route her devious mind would come up with next if he didn't clip her wings. Stripping off the climbing harness, he turned to Marshall. "Collect the gear and head back to your room. You're done for the night. Good job."

White teeth flashed in the dark. "Thanks, Major."

With an expert flick of his wrist Marshall brought the rope clattering down. The soldier quickly coiled the rope, and Griff collected the climbing gear from the balcony floor and handed it to Cash. Juliana rescued and gear collected they headed in out of the storm.

"Cash, tell Matt Ms. Bondevik can sleep with her door open tonight so he can make sure she doesn't leave this room. And have some of the men clear out the storage room down the hall. She can stay in there for the next nine days."

Standing next to her bed, Juliana gasped at his words. "You can't keep me in a *closet*."

He shot her a dark look. "Storage *room*. And, yes. I can keep you there. Be glad I'm not having you thrown in the brig. There's one here, you know. Beneath the sanctuary." And about now, he wouldn't mind having her tossed in the musty place. With fear still pounding an uneven beat in his heart and his groin aching with need, the brig sounded like a damned safe place for her.

Cash tipped his head toward Juliana. "Do you want me to stay with Ms. Bondevik until Matt gets here?"

Griff shook his head. "I'm sure he'll be here shortly. And in the meantime I'm going to have a little chat with the chancellor's daughter."

Cash squelched a smile. "I figured you might. I'll be in my office if you need me." Without another word, he and Marshall left the room, closing the door behind them.

Griff turned to Juliana, heated words racing to his tongue. But they died the second he looked at her.

She hadn't moved from her post by the bed. She

still stood there, shivering. But she wasn't huddled in on herself anymore. Now she stood tall, her chin tipped in defiance, her shoulders pulled back in challenge...and every square inch of her drenched clothing clinging to her like a second skin.

Holy good night.

Her tailored silk pants clung to her easy curves, accentuating the feminine roundness of her thighs and drawing his eye to the sweet delta of her womanhood. With Herculean effort he dragged his gaze upward. But there was no relief there. The soft, pink cotton sweater she'd probably thought would protect her from the night's chill, was sucked against her skin like shrink wrap. And her nipples, hard from the cold, pushed against the sodden material in bold relief.

He swallowed into a dry throat, the lecture he'd planned scattering like debris after a bomb blast. Blood poured to his groin. Old memories poured into his head. Memories of Juliana naked, in his bed, her soft skin gilded by the firelight. Her nipples hard, as they were now, but not from the cold. No, hard with passion, pouting for his touch.

He spun away, his fists clenched, need roaring through him. Closing his eyes, he blocked the enticing picture from his mind and forced the one from mere minutes before into its place. The picture of Juliana hanging from the chimney on his roof.

He turned back to her and jabbed an accusatory finger at the French doors. "What the hell were you trying to do out there? Break your neck?" His voice was predictably rough, but he managed to inject a fair amount of righteous indignation as well.

"What do you care?" she snapped, pain and anger filling her eyes. But she didn't give over to the tumultuous emotions. She quickly collected herself, pulling her shoulders back in regal aplomb. "Oh, I forgot, if anything happens to me, you'll have to deal with my father and the king and the president of the United States. Poor boy."

Aching with need and soul-deep longing, he clenched his fists, anger hitting him like a two-ton mortar charge. The last thing he wanted to hear right now was how much he didn't care for her when he'd spent the entire evening thinking he'd sell his soul for a single touch. A single bloody *touch.*

He stalked across the room until they were nose-to-nose. "If you're putting yourself through this non-sense to get away from me because you think I used you, that I didn't really want *you,* you can stop it right now." He pulled her against him and brought his lips down on hers, hard and demanding.

He kissed her with all the longing he'd stored up for the past two years, and all the years before that, and he didn't want to stop with a kiss. He wanted to strip them both naked, pull her onto the bed and show her just how much he wanted her.

He tore his lips from her, pulling back and stepping away, before he gave into that savage need.

She stared at him. Wide-eyed. Openmouthed. Stunned.

Which only egged him on. "I wasn't playing a game in the Alps. I meant every word, every damned touch. But there are demons in my life I don't want anywhere near you. I'm sorry for the way I left. I'm *sorry.* But there's not a damned thing I can do about it now.

"If you're angry with me, and you want to take it out on my hide, fine. Have Talon bring you to the gym tomorrow. You can have all the free shots you want. But if you put yourself in danger one more time, I won't be putting you in a comfy little room. I *will* be throwing your cute little butt in the brig." Without another word—before he made a bigger mess of this than he already had—he strode out of the room, signaled for Matt to take up his post by the door and headed down to his study. His study and the waiting bottle of Jack.

Juliana stared after Griffon's retreating figure, the blood rushing in her ears, her lips tingling with heat. His kiss had been hot and hard and greedy. And his want had been pressed up hard against her belly, proof that he might—just might—have meant his words.

I wasn't playing a game in the Alps. I meant every word, every damned touch. But there are demons in my life I don't want anywhere near you.

Demons? *What* was that about?

And did he really think he could dump that on her and then walk away?

She started after him.

But Matt stepped in front of her as she approached the open door, his expression grim. "Not tonight, Ms. Bondevik."

She stared at the behemoth.

He stared back, hard and unblinking.

Okay, not tonight. But if Griffon thought he could kiss her like that, hard and hungry, and talk about demons without answering for it...he needed a big-time reality check. And tomorrow she was going to give it to him.

Chapter Six

Juliana stared at the marked-up walls of the storage room. Griffon's men had spent the night cleaning it out—she'd heard them as she'd paced furiously around her room. And then Matt had moved her here early this morning.

It was a small windowless, escape-proof room. Big enough for a twin-size bed and nothing else. Not nearly big enough to get a good pace going. But right now that was the least of her worries. It had been a long, sleepless night filled with frustration and questions and uncertainty.

She'd spent the past two years thinking of Griffon Tyner as a user. And just because he'd kissed her and spouted some nonsense about demons last night didn't mean he wasn't. But...

What if it did?

What if there were extenuating circumstances that had led to his hasty departure? What then? How would that tiny bit of knowledge impact her life? Impact Perry's life?

She shook her head. After an entire night of mental wrangling, she had far more questions than answers. The only thing she knew for sure was that she had a right to know if Griffon was telling the truth. Had he left her at the lodge because something in his life had compelled him to? Or was that just another line to solicit her compliance?

She wanted to know. *Needed* to know. And to that end, she and Griffon were going to have a "little chat" as he so quaintly liked to call their discussions. Providing she could find something to put on. She *wasn't* wearing a dress to the gym. She rifled through her luggage, tossing dress after dress in first one direction and then the other. She'd managed to find the dress pants and cotton sweater for last night's escape, surely there were a few other practical things in this bag.

A couple more delicate designer labels hit the pile of discarded options, but finally she came to a small stash of tight capri pants...and shorty tops. She rolled her eyes. Not ideal, but they'd have to do.

She pulled the pants and top on, but she didn't bother with shoes. Her tennies were still wet from last night, and she would slit her throat before she'd put on a pair of heels with the tight pants and midriff-baring top. The sex-kitten look just wasn't her style.

She ran a quick brush through her hair and knocked on her door. Her *locked* door. After last night's escape, Griffon's men were now going all out to make sure she didn't pull another fast one.

She heard a key being fitted into the lock and the mechanism turning. Finally the door swung open. Talon stood in the doorway, a brow cocked in question. He didn't say anything, of course, heaven forbid he should break his vow of silence. He just stood there with a look of question on his arrogantly chiseled face.

She gave him an irritated huff. "I want to see Griffon."

"I'll talk to him and get back to you."

Her eyes popped wide. "You *do* speak."

He gave her a laconic look. "Of course I do." He closed the door.

She made a face at the oak panel as she heard his footsteps recede and the static of the radio. Good. He was calling Griffon.

Not thirty seconds later he knocked on her door and then opened it. "He's in the gym. He said to bring you down." He offered nothing more as he headed down the hall.

Scowling at his back, she followed him, watching his long black hair swing against his broad shoulders. The silky mass was really quite gorgeous. As was the man. Too bad all those good looks were attached to such a...a...stick.

She strode up beside him, his silence grating on her already frayed nerves. There were times when she wanted nothing more than to be ignored and treated like a normal person, not the chancellor's daughter, but now wasn't one of those times. "So tell me,

Talon, is this silence thing a vow? Or a zen thing? Or are you just afraid if you fraternize with the prisoner you might let your guard down?''

Silence reigned as she strode beside him.

She shook her head. ''All righty, then, we'll just say it's the latter. Since that's the most *polite* answer I can come up with. How's that?''

He didn't say anything, but a slight smile tugged at his lips and his black eyes twinkled.

She shook her head again. Naturally, the man would have a warped sense of humor. With his silent arrogance, how could he possibly have anything else?

Giving up on conversation, she followed him down the two sets of stairs, the cool marble chilling her feet, her stomach tight with apprehension. She didn't know what she hoped to learn in this little tête-à-tête. Or what she was going to do with the information if she managed to get any. She just knew she had questions she wanted answered. When they hit the entrance hall they made a sharp turn and headed toward the east wing.

She shot Mr. Silence a questioning look. ''Are we heading to the church? I thought we were going to the gym.''

''Patience, you're almost there.''

Like her father, patience had never been one of her virtues. And she was in no mood to add it today. But she didn't bother to comment as she followed him down the hall to two giant, dark mahogany doors. Definitely the church. She couldn't imagine these doors leading anywhere but the sanctuary.

She stepped back as Talon pulled the heavy doors

open. And sure enough, the sanctuary opened up before them, the arched ceiling soaring to dizzying heights, the giant stone pillars stretching up and up and up. Colored light spilled into the room from the stained-glass windows gracing both sides of the long, intricately designed room, their tales of biblical lore and brotherly love staring down at her. Beautiful, despite the fact it had been turned into a...

Gym.

She shook her head and strode into the giant chamber. All but a few pews had been ripped out, and red mats had been moved in to cover the hard stone floor. Punching bags, weight machines and bench presses littered the sides of the open chamber while a large space had been left in the middle for hand-to-hand combat. Two men fought there now, their gloved hands and padded feet connecting against flesh and bone with quick, hard thuds that reverberated in the high ceilings.

She winced and looked away from the violence. She hadn't come down here to see two men beat each other into the ground. She'd come down to find Griffon. And it didn't take long to do that.

He was working out near one of the stained-glass windows, his fists pummeling the heavy bag in a fast, punishing rhythm.

She walked over to him, glad her bare feet were on the red mats instead of the cold stone. She drew a breath to call his name.

But before she had the chance, he turned to her, holding his red-gloved hands wide. "Come to collect your due?"

Not in the manner he expected. But, yes, she'd come to collect her due. She met his gaze head on. "Absolutely."

Griffon turned to Talon, told him to wait in the hall and then he addressed the gym at large, canting his head toward the open doors. "Gentlemen."

Without so much as a word or even a hint they'd been inconvenienced, every man collected his gear and headed out of the gym. It was a credit to Griffon's leadership that they deferred to him so easily. She'd seen her father and the king command as much action with a single word—without causing dissension in the ranks—but few other men. She'd be impressed if she didn't know Griffon was capable of some pretty low behavior.

She watched the last of the men saunter out and then turned back to Griffon, raising a brow in question. "What? You don't want them to see a woman getting in her licks?"

His lips twisted wryly. "That hadn't occurred to me. But now that you mention it…"

He was standing so close she could feel his heat, see the sweat beading his skin, smell the spicy aftershave that would always remind her of his warm skin and his ardent touch and his keen passion.

Not the thoughts she needed to be thinking right now. She shook her head and turned away, concentrating on the pain that had seared her the morning she'd found him gone. Concentrating on what she saw around her. A mercenary stronghold.

She turned back to him. "This is an interesting

choice for a gym—and a place to practice the arts of war. The church.''

He raised a brow. ''Guess I don't have to look too hard for the censure there, do I? You think practicing war in a house of God is barbaric.''

''Isn't it?'' she challenged. After all, a mercenary stronghold was not the place one expected to find the most honorable of men. And she needed to know if Griffon Tyner was honorable—or as she'd suspected over the last two years—something less.

He looked around the room and shrugged. ''I think it's imminently appropriate. The stained-glass windows and high arched ceilings remind us all that at the heart of our battles we're not fighting for the sake of savagery but for the peace and brotherhood these windows depict. We need those reminders sometimes when we're heading into a nasty campaign. Or have just come home from one.''

They seemed to be the words of a commander who bled for his men and the victims—innocent and guilty alike—that war pulled into its ugly path. A soldier who fought not for the bloodlust of the battlefield, but for the small peace that victory brought. They seemed to be the words of a man who thought deeply. Felt deeply.

But were they words of truth, or merely pretty phrases spun together to impress her? ''That all sounds very benevolent. But hard to believe from a man who uses physical punishment within these same walls to keep your men in line.''

His brows snapped together in question. ''And you're referring to?''

"You told Matt if he didn't have a good excuse for my escape over the fence he was going to spend the next week doing hand-to-hand combat with Talon."

"Ah, that." He dismissed her concern with a negligent shrug. "I was beginning to wonder if you'd uncovered a torture chamber lurking in the shadows somewhere that I'd overlooked."

She raised an imperious brow. "And having one man pound another into the ground is any better?"

He sighed tiredly, stripping his boxing gloves off. "Maybe not. But there are consequences in life for screwing up. And this is a military installation, not summer camp. Keeping discipline is imperative. People's lives depend on it. My *men's* lives depend on it. And having them pay their penalties in the ring makes them think twice about screwing up again. *And* hones their fighting skills. Besides, shall I remind you that you came down here to do your own violence."

She shook her head. "No, I didn't. Hitting you isn't going to make me feel better. I came down here to talk to you." She met his gaze head on. "I want to hear about the demons."

His turn to shake his head. "Not up for discussion. You want to pound me to pulp, have at it. But that's all I'm offering."

She stared at him. "Does that mean you're denying there are demons? That you really had no ulterior motives for leaving that night? That you left for exactly the reason I always believed drove you from the hotel? You'd had your little fling, and leaving in the middle of the night was the quickest and easiest way to avoid a messy scene.'' She tried to keep the bitterness from her voice. But it was there, unmistakable and raw.

His lips pressed into a thin line, and he leaned toward her, his breath caressing her cheeks, his dark-green gaze sparking with anger. ''What we had at the lodge *wasn't* a fling. A mistake in judgement on my part during a moment of weakness, yes. But it wasn't a fling. For either of us.''

Her breath caught in her throat. His gaze was so intense, so direct, it seemed as if he were telling the truth. And part of her, the tenderest part of her, the saddest part of her, wanted to believe him. Was desperate to believe him. But the part of her that still ached with pain and regret was not about to believe him so easily.

She kept her gaze locked on his. ''I want to know why, Griffon. If you left me at the lodge for a good reason, I want to know what it was.''

The line of his lips got a little thinner. ''It won't change anything.''

''Maybe not. But I have a right to know.'' I have the right to know if that two weeks was real or a sham. I have a right to know if our daughter was conceived in love—or something less.

Dark shadows clouded his eyes. Dark, sad, troubled shadows. But before she had time to study them, to plumb their depths, he spun away, tossing his boxing gloves on a nearby bench. When he turned back, his gaze was unreadable, his expression an inscrutable mask. ''I don't have anything to tell you.''

She stared at him, long and hard.

He stared back, determined and resolute.

Damn him. She searched for another avenue of approach. "Has it ever occurred to you that if I thought you weren't a womanizing bastard, that if I thought you weren't a user, I might not be trying so hard to escape? That I'd be content to sit these two weeks out until the protests are over. Make everyone's lives easier?"

He flinched when she called him a womanizing bastard and a user, and something flashed in his eyes—something that might have been regret—but he blinked and the emotion disappeared. Now he simply raised a brow. "Threatening another escape?"

"Maybe," she goaded.

"From your storage room? Your *locked* storage room. Good luck."

Arrrgh. She'd momentarily forgotten her new quarters. Scowling, she searched for another way to get beyond his defenses. Her gaze slipped to his shoulder as she thought, catching on the tattoo there. A Liberty Bell with blood dripping from its famous crack.

She remembered the tattoo clearly from their time together in the lodge. She'd been fascinated by the way hard muscle had rippled beneath its colored lines. She'd asked about it then, asked if it stood for anything and when he'd gotten it. But he'd just shrugged the question off, saying it was nothing. That he'd gotten it one night when he'd been young and left his good sense in a bottle. Now, knowing the man's occupation, she suspected that had just been another lie.

She tipped her head toward the skin art. "That's

not something you did when you were drunk one night, is it? It's your company's insignia.''

His brows pulled together in a dark frown, but he nodded.

"So what name goes with that clever little icon?''

"Freedom Rings.''

She rocked back on her heels, recognizing the name immediately. "Freedom Rings?'' she squeaked, surprise and awe sliding through her. "It was your band that sneaked into the Palestinian stronghold and rescued Senator Arnold's little girl.''

His lips twisted unhappily, but he gave her a succinct nod. "Yes.''

She shook her head, trying to grasp the information that had just been dropped in her lap. She'd heard more than one story about Freedom Rings from her father and her country's chief of military. Some of the stories gloried in triumph and others wallowed in despair and defeat, but one fact was undisputed. "You're heroes,'' she breathed.

His lips twisted wryly. "A minute ago we were all barbarians. Now we're all heroes? Which is it?''

She ran her hand through her hair. "I don't know. I'm trying to figure it out.''

He shook his head. "Well, stop figuring. We're neither. We're just...dogs of war. Men with nothing but time on our hands and a grudge to grind against the unjust powers that be. Plain and simple.''

There wasn't anything simple about it. For her or Perry.

If she'd been wrong about the kind of man Griffon was, if he wasn't a scoundrel but a man of integrity and honor, a man who thought he was protecting her by keeping her out of his life, what then? Did she have a duty to tell him of his daughter? Would a man who'd risked his life to save another man's child want to know his own?

And what about Perry? If Griffon was a good man, wouldn't Perry want to know him? Didn't she have the right to know him?

Frustration pounded at her temples. If he would just tell her why he'd left two years ago—providing there was a legitimate reason—maybe then she'd know what to do. But he wasn't going to tell her. Not today. It was in the hard, determined look in his eyes, the stubborn set of his jaw and the rigid line of his shoulders.

He might never tell her.

And then what would she do?

Griff watched Juliana stride out the door, meet Talon and head back to her room. He cursed the fates for ever introducing them in the first place. And he cursed himself, for his own foolish weakness two years ago. And his inability to let go of those precious memories today.

All he had to do to was come clean, tell Juliana why he'd left her in the middle of the night. Tell her what kind of man he really was. Once she knew he'd have to come up the evolutionary scale several species to be the womanizing bastard she believed him to be—that he was anything but the hero she was beginning to think he was from the stories she'd heard about Freedom Rings—she'd be happy as a clam that he'd left her when he had.

She'd realize she was lucky to have him out of her world. She'd write their affair off as a bad experience and a lesson well learned and get on with her life. The sadness would leave her eyes, be replaced by disgust and contempt that would make her current anger pale by comparison. And that disgust and contempt would eventually fade into hard-learned wisdom.

But he couldn't do it.

He couldn't tell her what he really was. Facing the hate he saw in her eyes because she thought he'd used her was one thing. But facing the contempt he'd see once she knew what he really was, was something else all together. *That* he couldn't face.

He never should have taken that cup of hot chocolate from her in Switzerland. But he'd done it, anyway. And her laughter and beauty and gentleness had filled his soul. Filled his soul and replenished his will to go on. And he was still living off those memories. Without them there would be nothing left to get up for or fight for or breathe for. He couldn't let them go.

And for that sin, the fires of hell would burn the hottest.

Chapter Seven

With the exception of bathroom breaks, Juliana hadn't been allowed out of the storage room since yesterday morning when she'd spoken with Griffon. She wanted to pound the walls and scream in frustrated indignity. But she settled for stalking over to the locked door and giving it a good, swift kick. "Talon, let me out of here. Right now. I want to talk to Griffon."

Only silence greeted her from the other side of the door.

She scowled at the closed portal. "Call him again, Talon. Tell him I want to speak to him *now*."

More silence.

She kicked the door again, pain shooting up her toes. "*Talon.*"

A put-upon sigh whispered through the door. "The

last time I called, Ms. Bondevik, he said not to call again. If he thinks you need to see him, he'll send for you.''

Growling her indignation, she stalked away from the heavy oak panel. She could just picture the silent man on the other side. Smiling. Clenching her fists, she tried to pull her thoughts into some kind of order. But it wasn't any more possible this morning than it had been all day yesterday or all night last night. She didn't have enough information. She didn't have the one piece of information she needed.

Why Griffon had left her.

She was beginning to have doubts he'd left because he'd been trying to avoid an ugly and tiresome good-bye. A playboy's worst nightmare. But she didn't know for sure. And she *had* to know for sure before she allowed Perry anywhere near him. And if Griffon Tyner thought he could fob her off, he could think again.

She strode to the door and raised her fist, preparing to pound on the door when two sharp knocks reverberated through the storage room. She jumped, startled.

''I'm opening up, Ms. Bondevik. Griffon says to bring you downstairs.'' Talon's voice carried over the sound of jangling keys and the turning lock.

When the door swung open, she gave her keeper a dark scowl. ''It's about time.''

He lifted a brow at her acerbic tone, and his lips twisted in their usual bout of private humor, but he said nothing. He merely headed down the hall, leaving her to stay or follow as she chose.

With an irritated huff she strode after him, stretching her stride until she walked beside him. "You know, a little civil conversation wouldn't kill you. In fact, a little civil behavior in this place, period, would be a welcome addition."

She got a look this time that clearly said if she'd experienced anything less than civil behavior it was her own fault.

As if *he* would have sat idly by if someone had kidnapped him. With a shake of her head she walked silently beside him, her mind back on the dilemma at hand. Getting Griffon to talk. Soon. Before her father decided to take matters into his own hands and tell Griffon about Perry.

Of course, if Griffon did talk, and she decided she'd made the right choice in the first place—that she didn't want him in Perry's life—she didn't know what she was going to do. She wasn't getting out of that storage room. And if her father's patience was wearing as thin as hers, disaster was right around the corner.

She pushed that unnerving thought away and padded alongside Talon down the wide marble staircase to the second floor. As always their footsteps echoed in the empty halls. A tiny shiver ran through her. She couldn't imagine living in a place so quiet...so lonely.

The emptiness of the place bordered on complete isolation. Why on earth would Griffon want to live here? For all its opulence and glory, the place reminded her of a mausoleum. If she were him, she'd be staying at that cute little cabin in the woods. At least one wouldn't seem quite so alone there. The rough-hewn walls would be close, comforting, like a warm blanket, as opposed to the impersonal walls here that seemed miles away and as cold as the North Sea.

Or if the cabin didn't appeal, why didn't he have a half dozen or more house guests wandering around? Her lips twisted. Or if he was a womanizing scoundrel, several of his girlfriends? Didn't he know a person's house should be full of people? Family. Friends. *Anyone.* She might even welcome an enemy or two into these silent, echoing hallways.

Halfway down the staircase to the main floor she noticed Griffon waiting for them in the foyer below. He looked as lonely as his halls, standing there in the giant foyer, dressed in his camo fatigues, black T-shirt and heavy, lace-up boots.

Lonely...and handsome. Handsome and strong and...stubborn.

Steeling herself for whatever he had in mind, she stepped off the bottom step, strode over to him and met his gaze head-on. "Did you bring me down here to talk? Or have you decided the storage room isn't secure enough and you're dragging me off to the brig?"

His lips twisted wryly. "Neither. Your father called to say a car with a present for you will be arriving any minute. I thought you'd want to be here to receive it."

A present? There was only one thing that package could be. Panic exploded in her head. "I don't want it. Tell the guard at the gate to refuse the car and send it back.'' The words came out in a rush, her heart aching at the lie. But she wouldn't take it back. For Perry's sake she couldn't.

Griffon's brows crashed together. ''Why don't you want it?''

She scrambled for a reason that sounded legitimate. ''The last thing my father did was have me *kidnapped*. What makes you think whatever is in that car is any better?'' It was better. Way better. She'd sell her soul for what her father had sent all the way from the North Sea. But she wouldn't sell Perry's soul for it. No way. Not if there was even a chance Griffon was the user she'd originally thought he was. ''Send it back.''

Watching her, he snatched the radio from the wide belt at his waist and lifted it to his lips, depressing the talk button. ''Ragston,'' he barked into the unit.

The radio crackled to life as Griffon released the button. ''Sir?''

''When Chancellor Bondevik's car arrives, hold it at the gate until further notice.''

The radio crackled again. ''Sorry, Major. I just passed it through. It's pulling up to the front of the mansion as we speak. Is there something wrong? Should I send men up?''

Griffon looked to Juliana, a single brow cocked in question.

She quickly shook her head. The last thing she wanted were a bunch of guns and trigger-happy soldiers around that car.

Griffon punched the talk button again. ''Not now. But keep a sharp eye. Any sign of trouble, send them running.'' His gaze never leaving hers, he clipped the radio back on his belt and waved a hand toward the door. "Shall we?"

She rushed ahead of him, praying she could head this disaster off at the car. She wasn't sure how she'd head it off, but something would occur.

Talon beat them both to the door, pulling one of the heavy panels open for them.

She strode out of the giant portal, Griffon hard on her heels. The long, black limo had already pulled up at the edge of the stone veranda. Her heart leaped into her throat, strangling her and making it impossible to breathe. The driver was already out...and opening one of the wide back doors. *No, don't get out. Go home,* she wanted to yell, but only a strangled sound came out. And then it was too late. Edward, her father's secretary, was getting out.

With Perry in his arms.

Her heart stopped. The world froze and then slipped into slow motion. Perry was wearing a fancy pink dress of dotted Swiss chiffon with a million ruffles. A matching headband circled her tiny head, making her short blond hair stick out in spikes. And lastly, her small, kicking feet were clad in white-patent leather shoes with ruffly socks peeking out of the top.

Juliana's heart wrenched. She wanted to snatch her baby from Edward's arms and hug her tight. But she wanted to protect that tiny little heart, too. And that meant getting her back in that car and on her way out of this compound before Griffon had a chance to give her a good look.

If he didn't get any closer maybe she could fob

Perry off as a distant cousin or some such thing. But if he got a good look…he'd know.

She forced a breath into her lungs to tell Edward to get in that car and get out of here. Now. But before the first words left her lips, Perry saw her.

The tiny girl startled, surprised to see Juliana. And then her cherubic face broke into a huge grin, an excited shriek sliced the crisp morning air, and tiny arms reached for her.

All was lost. Juliana could have sent Perry away if her daughter had never seen her. Could have sent her away knowing Perry missed her and probably wondered what had happened to her mommy. She could have sent her away because Juliana knew it was for the best. At least until she found out for sure who Griffon Tyner was. But there was no way she could send her away now. No way.

She rushed to her daughter and gathered her in her arms. Tears stung her eyes as tiny arms wrapped around her neck and squeezed tight. Juliana hugged back, the tiny little body feeling so perfect as it snuggled against her, the smell of baby powder filling her nose.

Exuberant gurgles tumbled through the air as Perry wiggled in her arms. Juliana held her tight, whispering a Bjorlian hello in her tiny, shell-shaped ear and following it with a string of endearments. She'd missed her so much.

But this was not a perfect reunion. In fact, it could be a very dangerous reunion. She glanced to Griffon.

He stared at them, then looked back to the car as if expecting the baby's mother to get out at any moment. But when no one else emerged from the vehicle, his gaze snapped to Perry. He looked at her fair hair and then at Juliana's as realization began to dawn. "She's yours." His voice was strained, rough.

Her arms tightened around her squirming daughter. "Yes."

He looked back to Perry, alarm flashing in his eyes as he no doubt did quick mathematical calculations in his head, adding and subtracting to come up with a general conception date. His eyes narrowed infinitesimally.

Perry turned in her arms, looking at Griffon with interest.

His gaze caught and settled on Perry's eyes.

Eyes the color of mountain pines.

His own deep-green eyes went wide. The color drained from his skin, and he drew a sharp, hard breath.

Lord help her.

He knew.

Pain, dark and deep, slashed across Griff's soul, and the world tilted under his feet. He rocked back a step.

Juliana stepped forward, sudden concern knitting her brow, one hand reaching out as if to steady him. "Griffon?"

He shook his head, stepping away from her touch. Clenching his fists, he stared at Perry, tension vibrating in every molecule of his body.

A baby.

A tiny, helpless—defenseless—baby.

His baby.

Dear God.

Cold sweat coated his skin. A lifetime of being careful, an adulthood of denial so he could ensure that the violence of his childhood would not contaminate one more family, would not hurt one more person, scar one more child, and he'd blown all that effort in two short weeks. In one moment of weakness.

He stared at the tiny child. At her cherub's smile and her bright-green eyes. His heart hitched, squeezing in his chest, refusing to beat in a normal rhythm. He shifted his gaze to Juliana. Sweet, giving Juliana with a dull, aching sadness in her eyes. A sadness he'd put there.

The fires of hell licked at his heels. And his father's vicious laughter echoed in his ears. God, what had he done? Had he put into motion events that would drive Juliana and the tiny baby and himself into the life he'd fought so hard to get out of? His stomach turned, and his hands shook. He couldn't let it happen. *He couldn't.*

But how the hell would he prevent it now?

He turned away from Juliana and his baby. Turned away and strode toward the steps leading to the road. He had to get out of here. Get out of here and get to a place where he could think. Before it was too late.

Chapter Eight

Juliana smiled down at Perry as she taped a fresh diaper into place. They were back in her original room with its plush carpets and fancy furniture. She'd made it clear this morning that she wasn't keeping her daughter in a storage room or allowing her anywhere near that closet's filthy floor. And since there would obviously be no more worries about her escaping—she would hardly climb onto the roof with her baby—she'd demanded Talon return them here.

And the man had obviously seen the reason in her argument, because he'd brought her here with no fuss, directing a few of Griffon's men to collect her items from the storage room.

Snatching up the clean dress she'd taken from Perry's luggage, she slid chubby arms into the small, puffed sleeves and buttoned the tiny mother-of-pearl buttons running down the front.

Perry kicked her feet as if she objected to the fancy attire.

Juliana gave her a wry smile, finishing up the last button. "I know, pants are so much better for crawling around on the floor. But Theresa packed as impractically for you as she did for me. All satin and silk and froo-froo dresses." She gave her head a disgusted shake. "She's in cahoots with your grandpa, you know."

As if Perry understood every word, she made an unhappy face, clenched her tiny hands in fists and shrieked an outraged squeal.

Juliana laughed. "Yeah. That's kind of how I feel about Grandpa right now, too. We can both strangle him when we get home. Come on." Scooping her daughter from the bed, Juliana gave her a giant hug. It was good to have her in her arms again. "Love you, sweetie pie." With a final squeeze, she placed her on the light-blue carpet and set her free.

Perry crawled away at top speed, heading straight for the open suitcase. Once there, she crawled in and started tossing its contents out. Clothes, toys, diapers.

Juliana smiled as she dropped onto the cushy four-poster bed to watch. Fun stuff.

Perry smiled and gurgled with delight, tossing one item after the other out of the beige leather bag.

Juliana wanted that smile to last forever. Wanted Perry to always be as happy as she was right now.

But that happiness was in serious jeopardy.

Tension drew Juliana's nerves tight. Over the past

two years, she'd often wondered how Griffon would react if he found out he had a daughter.

She'd thought irritation or disgust would be his initial reaction. Those were emotions she imagined a user might feel when he discovered he had an unwanted baby. And she'd expected those emotions to be followed by cool calculation. Griffon wondering how best to use his daughter's position to his advantage. But Juliana hadn't seen either of those emotions. She'd seen raw, naked fear in his eyes. Where had that come from?

She drew in a deep breath, and then another, trying to calm her own racing fears. Her father had taken the decision of whether or not to let Griffon know he had a daughter out of her hands, but the decision to let Griffon into Perry's life or close him out altogether was still firmly within her grasp. If she decided Griffon's existence in her daughter's life would only bring unhappiness and misery and she told her father *that,* he'd be right beside her with all his lawyers and all his power to make sure Griffon never saw his daughter again.

But she wasn't at all certain Griffon's presence in Perry's life would be a mistake anymore. And keeping him away from his daughter was a decision she would not make lightly. Every child had a right to her father's love. And every father had a right to his daughter's. Providing he didn't ruin his daughter's life to get it.

She stared at Perry, her heart aching, her nerves raw with the unknown. She wanted everything beautiful and wonderful and bright for her daughter, and right now she didn't have a clue what that was.

And she wasn't going to figure it out sitting in this room.

She pushed herself up from the bed and crossed to Perry, who was hiding a bright orange-and-blue ball under all the clothes she'd pulled from the luggage. "Come on, sweetie pie, let's go see what your daddy has to say for himself."

Griffon might not be any more amenable to answering her questions now than he had been before Perry showed up. But if Perry was with her, perhaps Juliana could see some indication of what he was thinking in his expression. The eyes were supposed to be the windows to the soul. What man could look at his newly found daughter and not show some honest feeling in his eyes?

She scooped Perry into her arms.

With a happy whoop, Perry dived toward her, her warm cuddly body crashing into Juliana's chest, her tiny arms wrapping tightly around her neck. Juliana breathed deeply. Fresh skin and baby powder. Smiling, she settled her baby comfortably in the crook of one elbow and made her way to the door. She twisted the knob experimentally. Unlocked. Good. Without hesitation or permission she pulled the door open.

But Talon was there immediately, blocking her exit, a single brow cocked in question.

She scowled at him. "I want to see Griffon. Right now."

Talon's expression clearly said she'd better not count on her wants being met anytime soon.

But she was in no mood to take no for an answer. And there was no way he was going to fight with her with Perry in her arms. She dropped a shoulder and pushed by him into the hall. And she didn't stop there. She bee-lined for the stairs.

"Hey." Talon was immediately beside her, his long stride easily matching hers. "You can't just leave your room and go barging in on Griffon unannounced and uninvited."

She stopped and faced him, Perry held boldly in front of her, making it clear she was well aware there was nothing he would do as long she was holding her baby. "Of course I can. Who's going to stop me?"

His black eyes narrowed on her. "You fight dirty, Ms. Bondevik."

"You think being the chancellor's daughter is all about charity luncheons and learning how to hold your pinky just so when you sip a cup of tea?" She raised an imperious brow. "Did you know that over the last four hundred years, the Bondeviks have raised arms over eighty times to protect the Monrad monarchy?"

"No. I didn't know that."

"Did you know that in 1897 my great-grandmother beheaded a conquering soldier who put the ten-year-old prince of Bjorli in danger? Do you think she would have done any less for her own child? Do you think I would do any less for mine?"

His lips twisted with humor. "Are you planning to behead me? Or Griffon? If it's me, be warned, I'm rather fond of my head. And if it's Griffon, you are biting off more than you can chew. No one here will allow it. Least of all Griffon.''

"Let's hope I don't have to get that drastic then. But if Griffon thinks I'm going to let him lock us in a room while he decides at his own leisure just what part he wants to play in his daughter's life, he's wrong. And if you think I won't fight you right here, right now, to preserve my daughter's rights and ensure her happiness, you're wrong, too.''

His lips quirked again, and humor leaped from his eyes.

But whether his amusement was directed at Griffon or herself, she didn't know. And she didn't care, she was only greatly relieved when the enigmatic soldier waved a hand toward the stairs and said, "By all means then, let's go.''

Griff sat at his desk and stared blindly at the papers strewn before him. He was supposed to be going through requests for his company's services and deciding what situations deserved his men's commitment. But the only thoughts in his head were the ones he'd been wrestling with all day. Thoughts of Juliana and the baby who'd shown up on his veranda this morning.

Panic had all but blinded him then. He'd stalked off in a cold sweat, his head spinning. And somewhere between the mansion and the gates he'd started running.

The guards had opened the gate for him, allowing him to keep running across the valley floor and into the woods that covered the surrounding hills. He'd run for hours, pushing himself up the surrounding ridge, back down to the valley floor and back up again.

He'd run until his legs had given out and he'd collapsed against a big, rough-barked pine where he'd sat listening to the birds chirp and the insects buzz. And where he'd finally realized that maybe, just maybe, Juliana and that baby were a gift and not the biggest mistake of his life. Yes, he'd planned to live his life alone. But...Juliana was here. The baby was here. In fact, everything he'd ever wanted, ever hoped for, ever dreamed of, was right here in this house.

And there was just something about the sight of a man's child that made him want to believe anything was possible. That made him want to believe if he played his cards right, he just might be able to have some of his dreams. At least he had to try.

A knock on the door startled him out of his musings. He turned to the closed portal. "Come in."

The door opened and Talon leaned in. "Ms. Bondevik demanded to see you." A suspicious, humorous curve turned the man's lips.

Griff's own lips twitched. He was surprised she'd waited this long. "Let her in."

Talon began to move aside, but then leaned back in. "Cash said to let you know he replaced Matt as Ms. Bondevik's guard at Matt's request. Marshall will be taking the midnight shift from now on."

Griff grimaced. Matt Rutger was one of his best soldiers, but he had one major weakness. He couldn't bear to be around babies. It was a weakness the soldier would have to get over if he ever wanted to have his life back. But Griff didn't have time to worry about that right now. He had his own life to get in order. He gave Talon a short nod. "Fine. Show Ms. Bondevik in."

Talon moved aside and Juliana walked in. Carrying—God, he didn't even know her name.

The clock ticked in the suddenly intimate room. Griff stared at the tiny girl in Juliana's arms. She was garbed in a ruffly yellow dress with a delicate string of satin roses ringing the small neckline. Yellow, patent-leather shoes with matching roses covered her feet and the apparently requisite ruffled socks finished off the outfit. She looked cuter than a basket of puppies. And twice as curious. Her eyes—a smaller version of his own—stared at him with bright interest and burgeoning expectation.

His heart squeezed, and he shifted his gaze to Juliana. "What's her name?"

"Perry." The response was short and a little tense.

Not a surprise. If she'd meant to keep this baby's existence a secret—and she obviously had—her day had probably been as tumultuous as his. And she couldn't be any more certain of the direction their lives were about to take than he was. They had a lot to talk about. But they would address the adult matters later. Right now he was interested in his daughter.

Perry.

He cocked his head, studying the baby, not sure he liked the name choice. She was so tiny and delicate. Beautiful. And the name was so... "Isn't that a man's name?"

Juliana's chin tipped in defense. "It's a nick-name."

Ah. "What's her real name?"

Juliana's lips pressed together, as if she was uncertain just how much of her child's life she wanted to share with him. "Perry's all you need to know right now."

He raised a brow. "You don't think I have a right to know my own child's name?"

"I haven't decided yet."

"Now wait just a minute. You haven't decided?" He narrowed his gaze on her. "Listen, I did a lot of thinking this afternoon. And one of the things I realized was that while I made some mistakes at the lodge—one major one—I was not the only one keeping secrets."

Juliana's brows snapped together in confusion. "What is that supposed to mean?"

He gave her a pointed look. "Smith?"

A red flush colored her cheeks, and she had the grace to look away.

Yeah. Now she remembered.

She'd introduced herself to him at the lodge as Juliana Smith. Not Juliana Bondevik. Definitely not Juliana Bondevik, the daughter to the chancellor of Bjorli. Just plain old Juliana Smith. He didn't know why. Didn't know if she'd gone to Switzerland to hide from her life or just to slum it. He didn't know why she'd misrepresented herself. Only that she had. And that if he'd known she was the chancellor's daughter he never would have touched her. *Never.* And everyone would have been better off for it.

Everyone except the tiny girl in her mother's arms.

He shook his head. "Never mind. That's ancient history. Neither of us can change it." He looked at Perry, marveling at her existence. "I don't think either of us wants to change it. But I'm not going to take all the blame for what happened there anymore, either, Juliana. We were both there. We were both responsible. Just like we're both responsible for what happens from this point forward."

She nodded once. "We need to talk."

Yes, they did. He nodded, waving a hand toward his desk. "Have a seat."

She strode the short distance to the chair in front of the desk and lowered herself into it, her movements stiff and awkward, devoid of her usual easy grace.

He moved to his chair and sat with the same awkward stiffness.

They stared at each other across the paper-strewn desk between them, knowing they sat poised on a momentous decision. A decision that would affect their lives. Affect their daughter's life. Profoundly.

Perry squirmed for release now that Juliana was stationary.

He quickly looked around the office and then looked back to Juliana with a shrug. "You can put her on the floor. I don't think there's anything in here that can hurt her."

Juliana looked over the room, clearly distrustful of his judgment to decide what was safe and what was not. But after a careful sweep she obviously agreed with his assessment because she set her precious cargo down.

The little tyke crawled off, making excited baby noises, her eyes alight with mischief and adventure as she scoped out the new room.

God, had he ever been that innocent? He mentally shook his head. No. Not with his father in the house.

But he would do everything in his power to make sure this little girl knew nothing but smiles and praises and endless encouragement. He watched her crawl across the floor with such delighted exuberance.

His heart clenched. She was so damned...perfect. And eight hours ago he hadn't even known she existed. He closed his eyes, trying not to think about the things he'd already missed, trying not to think he might never have known he had a daughter. He looked back to Juliana.

She was watching him, her gaze sharp, intense. "I need to know why you left in the middle of the night, Griffon."

His gut tightened and he shook his head. "I thought we decided what happened then doesn't matter. We're here now. And we need to go on."

She shook her now. "You decided what happened then doesn't matter. But *I* need to know."

His palms broke into a cold sweat, and he tried to chase her away from the subject with a scowl. "It won't change anything."

She drew in a breath, her intense gaze never leaving his face. "It won't change what happened in the past, no. But I need to decide if I want you in Perry's life or not. And I think the answer to that question is key."

His gut twisted. He was under no misconceptions.

She had the power of a crown behind her. If she decided to make sure he never saw his daughter again, it would be one hell of a legal battle to change that scenario. And he'd undoubtedly lose.

Maybe he could give her part of the truth. A tiny part of it. "I left for the same reason I didn't tell you what I did in the first place. Because I'm a mercenary. Although my motives for not having you discover that fact changed over the time I knew you."

She narrowed her eyes. "What does that mean?"

"It means when I first met you I didn't want you to know what I did for a living because I knew how you would react. I knew the word *mercenary* would make you tuck tail and run."

She opened her mouth to protest, but he held his hand up to stop the first words from leaving her mouth. "Before you deny it, I'll remind you of the way you reacted the first day you were brought here and you found out what I did for a living. Remember?"

A light flush climbed into her cheeks and she looked away, no doubt remembering her nasty sneer when she'd discovered his occupation.

"Exactly my point. You would have tucked tail and run. And quite frankly, after the first five minutes of your smile I didn't want that to happen. Was it an unwise choice, an unfair choice? Probably. Am I sorry for it? I wish I could say yes. But I'm not sorry. Those two weeks were the best of my life."

And, damn him to hell, if those two weeks had resulted in the tiny, busy little girl pulling the books from the bottom shelf of his bookcase and tossing them hither and yon in delight, then he was damned glad for them. But none of that excused the way he'd ended it.

He grimaced. "As for the way I left. It was a coward's retreat. You were suddenly talking about extending the relationship beyond the lodge. Which meant I would have to tell you who I was. *What* I was—"

"I wouldn't have cared, Griffon. By then I wouldn't have cared."

His heart clenched. "I know, because by then, if I'd discovered you were Jane the Ripper it wouldn't have meant a damned thing to me, either. I would have still wanted you. And I was pretty sure you were as caught up in the affair as I was. Which is why I didn't tell you. Why I just left. I was afraid you would say it didn't matter, and I'd be too weak to send you packing. And then what was I going to do? Bring you here?" He injected the sheer ludicrousness of that idea into his tone.

Her brows snapped together in confusion. "What's wrong with here? It's a *mansion,* Griffon. Most little girls dream of marrying a rich man and ending up in a mansion."

His lips twisted in self-deprecation. "Beyond its architectural points this isn't a mansion, Juliana. It's a soldiers' *stronghold.* A place where men practice for war. You said so yourself in the gym the other morning." He shook his head. "And if I'd made a different decision I would have brought the chancellor's daughter to it."

Her lips turned down unhappily. Impatiently. "I'm

just a person, Griffon. I may be the chancellor's daughter, but I'm just a person.''

He shook his head, meeting her gaze squarely. "No you're not. You might wish you were sometimes, but you're not. Bringing you here would have been unconscionable."

Shadows flitted in Nordic blue, but he pressed on. "I'm sorry for the way I left. God, I'm sorry. But being sorry doesn't change the bottom line. This is no place for a woman. Or a child."

Her brows pulled together again. "So what are you saying? You don't want to be a part of your daughter's life?"

"No…" That's not what he was saying at all.

She splayed a hand in question. "Then what *are* you saying?"

His mind ground to a sudden halt. What the hell was he saying? This afternoon he'd realized that now that they were here, in his house, in his life, he wanted to be part of their lives. But he hadn't had time to think of what that might mean in practical terms. To any of them.

He swiveled in his chair, his gaze settling on Perry as his mind grappled with the looming problems.

He watched Perry turn the pages on a few of the books that had fallen open when she'd tossed them out of the bookshelves. The soft sound of riffling pages fluttered through the room. As though she sensed his attention, she looked up, a happy smile turning her lips. And then she crawled toward him, her expression alight with the adventure of getting to know someone new.

His heart thumped and ached at the same time.

She crawled steadily to him, her dress catching occasionally under her knees, stopping her and making her frown. But once she moved around enough to free the material she was on her way again. And then she was at his feet, grabbing his pants leg and pulling herself up.

He glanced to Juliana, a father's pride swelling in his chest. "She's standing."

Juliana nodded, the corners of her own lips turning up. "As long as she has something to hold on to."

She could always hold on to him. He looked back to Perry, smiling. "Hey pretty baby, what are you up to?"

Holding tight to his camos with one hand, she stretched the other up to him and chirped an unintelligible demand. But he knew what she wanted. He'd been the oldest of four kids; he was pretty savvy in baby-speak.

His throat went dry, and he looked over to Juliana. "Can I pick her up?"

She smiled ruefully. "I think you're going to hear about it if you don't."

He swallowed hard and scooped her up before he lost his nerve. He'd picked up babies a thousand times. A million times.

But that had been different.

This was *his* child.

His fingers flexed, sinking into soft yellow ruffles as he held on to Perry. She cooed and giggled and leaned toward him, batting playfully at his chest with her tiny hands.

She was so beautiful. So small. So fragile.

He remembered when his sister Emily was this small. Remembered holding her like this, late at night. Usually he was trying to keep her from crying so she wouldn't wake their father. Wouldn't incur—

A sudden chill ran down his spine. A chill spiked with reality. Dear God, what was he doing?

Back when he was holding his sister, taking care of her—taking care of both his sisters and brother— he'd known what kind of violence his father was capable of. Known how often his sire took his anger at life out on his wife and children with his fists. But Griffon hadn't known then that the same violence flowed in his own veins.

Back then he'd believed he would never lose his temper with anyone. Never touch anyone in violence. He was positive he wasn't going to be a mean son of a bitch like his old man, no way, no how.

An empty laugh echoed through his head. Had he been a fool. He was *just* like his old man. A lesson he'd learned when he was fifteen and his younger brother had pushed Griffon's buttons once too often.

He looked at his giant, rough hands next to Perry's delicate ones. Looked at his long, strong fingers wrapped around her tiny, fragile bones. Griff thought of his brother's bloody nose. The nose he'd broken all those years ago. He thought of all the battles he'd fought since.

He had only to think back to the battlefield he'd fought on a few weeks ago to know his temper hadn't changed a bit over the years. When he'd seen the carnage the South American soldiers had wreaked on that small town, his temper had snapped. He'd gone after those butchers like the hound of hell he was. None of those bastards would ever touch another woman or child again.

But he didn't have any business touching them, either.

His hands started to shake, and his chest ached, as if a tank were driving over it. What the hell had he been thinking this afternoon when he'd sat in the woods? Had he lost his mind? He couldn't be a part of his daughter's life. His father's blood ran far too strongly through his veins. He closed his eyes and tried to swallow, but the muscles in his throat refused to work.

He'd promised himself the day he'd hit Sean he'd never risk hurting anyone he loved again. And then he'd hit the streets, where he'd vowed to remain a solitary soul. Vowed never again to put himself in a position where he could hurt someone he loved.

And he wasn't about to break that vow now. Not with this bubbly little girl's future riding on it.

With a shaky hand he ran the back of his fingers over her tiny head, feeling the soft, silky cap of straight, blond hair. So beautiful. So like her mother's.

Something suspiciously like tears stung his eyes, but he blinked hard, forcing them back. He'd made the right decision twenty years ago. Remaining single, unattached was the only sane decision he could make. It might be ripping his heart out now, but it was the right decision. He ran his fingers down her hair again. Soft. Silky. Precious.

The tiny girl smiled, grabbed his finger, dragged it to her mouth and gnawed softly on it, her expression one of easy acceptance and complete trust.

A tear slipped past his defenses, but he flicked it away, as if it were an itch. Then he drew a deep, ragged breath and looked to Juliana. "Obviously, I didn't know what I was saying a few moments ago. But I do now."

He ran his fingers over Perry's hair once more, cherishing the feel of the silky strands. Reluctantly he lowered his hand. "You were right to keep her a secret from me. I don't belong in her life. And once you leave here I won't contact you again. Either of you. You'll be free to tell her whatever you want about me. It might be easiest if you just tell her I'm dead. I won't fight you on it."

Juliana stared at Griffon, relief pouring through her. Obviously, if he was proposing to bow out of Perry's life, he had no plans to use the child. But if bowing out of her life was causing him so much pain, why was he willing to do it? And there was definitely pain. She'd seen the tear.

He might think he'd fooled her by that I've-got-an-itch bit, but he hadn't. She cocked her head, watching him. He'd made sure no more than one rogue tear had escaped, and now he'd smoothed his expression into an emotionless mask, but she'd never seen so much sadness in a man's eyes.

So why on earth was he suggesting she tell Perry he was dead?

She raised a brow. "You're not interested in being in your daughter's life? Is that right?"

His lips thinned into a hard line. "I'm saying this isn't a place for children. And I can't think of a single reason to taint her otherwise fairy-tale life by sticking an old man who gets paid to kill people in the middle of it."

She huffed in exasperation. "You make yourself sound like an assassin."

"Her friends will think I am."

"As the granddaughter to the chancellor she probably won't have any friends. And if she did, if they were real friends, they wouldn't believe that of you."

He scowled at her. "Why are you fighting me on this? You've almost killed yourself twice trying to get away from me. And now you suddenly think I should be in our daughter's life?"

She shrugged. "I haven't decided anything yet. But I've learned a lot about you in the past few days, and I'm not at all certain Perry would be better off without you."

"You'll have to take my word for it, then."

She laughed humorlessly. "You don't really think I'm that easy do you?" If she thought for one second he was opting out of his daughter's life because he wasn't interested in being in it, she'd agree to his suggestion. But...

The aching sadness in his eyes, the gentle, almost reverent way he ran his fingers over his daughter's hair suggested he cared deeply for the life he'd created. So why was he trying to distance himself from her? "If you're so concerned your profession would embarrass her, or be bad for her, why don't you quit? Do something else?''

His expression hardened. ''Changing jobs isn't an option. I'm a soldier, Juliana. This is where I belong.'' He said it as if he were some kind of wild animal. As if he needed to be here, in this remote outpost, to keep society safe.

She cocked her head, studying him. It didn't make sense. Although he seemed sincere in what he said, the puzzle didn't quite fit together. She wasn't sure what pieces were missing, or if she was just trying to put the puzzle of Griffon Tyner together wrong. But she did know something was out of whack. ''I don't believe it, Griffon.''

He lifted a challenging brow. ''Don't believe what? That Perry would be better off without me?''

''That you think you wouldn't be a fit parent because of your profession. You're not ashamed of your profession. You told me so the first day I was here, remember? And I don't think you left me without saying goodbye because you didn't want to bring me back to a soldier's stronghold, either. I think both of those decisions have to do with your—'' she flexed the first two fingers of each hand in the air, simulating quotes ''—demons.''

A muscle along his jaw flexed.

Yep. She'd hit that nail on the head. She gritted her own teeth. ''I want to know what those demons are. And I'm not going to make a decision about you and Perry until I do.''

He looked away from her, the muscle in his jaw

flexing like a steady pulse now. But the only sounds in the room were Perry's soft coos.

Juliana huffed in exasperation. "You're not going to tell me, are you?"

"No."

She gave him an imperial shrug that she'd learned from the king of Bjorli. "Well, there you have it then. I guess we have an impasse. For now."

Chapter Nine

Juliana stood next to the bed, holding up the doll-size white dress with purple flowers for Perry's perusal. "Well, look at this, sweetie pie, *more ruffles.*"

Lying on the bed, looking up at her, Perry frowned and grabbed hold of the dress, her chubby legs kicking as her fingers squashed the crisp cotton. She didn't seem any happier with her fancy wardrobe today than she had the day before.

Juliana didn't blame her. As she stared down at the cranky baby in sympathy Perry gave a mighty yawn.

Juliana followed suit, yawning wide. Shaking her head, she pointed an accusatory finger at her. "That was your fault, you little monkey, keeping me up half the night. You think just because you flew halfway around the world yesterday to end up here in this strange house full of strange people you had a right to be cranky half the night?''

Totally oblivious to the complaint Perry pulled at the dress.

Juliana gently pulled it from her grasp. ''Oh no you don't. Like it or not, I've got to put this on you. Come on.'' She slipped the dress over Perry's head and then went to work, maneuvering busy arms into the sleeves. Another yawn assailed her.

She *was* tired but it wasn't all Perry's fault. While the grumpy baby had kept her up the first half of the night, worrying about how she was going to deal with Griffon had kept her up the rest of the night.

Despite her attempts to find out about Griffon's demons, he'd told her nothing. And she didn't think he was going to suddenly become more forthcoming in the future. Unless she found a way to twist his arm.

An approach she was more than willing to use.

Being the chancellor's daughter was a hard, lonely job. She didn't want to think about how much harder and lonelier it would have been without her mother and father's unquestioning love and support. Being the chancellor's granddaughter wouldn't be any easier. If Griffon had the capacity to love his little girl, it was too precious a commodity to let slip through their fingers. Far too precious.

But finding the leverage she'd need to twist his arm was going to be a challenge. She turned Perry over and snapped up the back of the frothy dress. ''Well, Perry girl, we've got our work cut out for us. But we're up for it, aren't we?'' She picked Perry up and gave her a conspiratorial smile. ''If your daddy thinks he can fob us off with some weak, vague excuse like demons, he's obviously never dealt with a couple of determined Bondeviks before, has he?''

Perry smiled back, grabbing Juliana's hair and giving it a tug.

''Okay, let's go.'' Settling Perry in her arms, she left the room.

Talon greeted her outside the door with his usual silent greeting. A lifted brow.

She gave him a determined smile. ''We're off to see Griffon. And if you pick that radio up and warn him, I'm going to have to set this baby down and wring your neck, so don't even think about it.''

The warrior's lips twitched and his eyes twinkled but he didn't say anything—or touch the radio at his belt—as he followed her.

They made their way down to the second floor and then down to the foyer where she turned left, toward Griffon's office.

Talon halted in his tracks. ''He's not in his office, Ms. Bondevik.''

She stopped and turned back to the silent warrior, preparing to drag the information out of him if she had to. ''Where is he?''

Talon struck off in the opposite direction. ''In his study. This way.''

She caught up, wondering briefly why he was being so cooperative. But she didn't dwell on the subject for long. She suspected the man just enjoyed watching others flounder. And she was glad she didn't have to fight her way to Griffon.

They hadn't gone too far before Talon stopped in front of a closed door.

She gave him a questioning look when he merely stood there. "You're not going to announce me?"

Dark eyes twinkled. "And ruin your surprise? Absolutely not."

She shook her head. "You're a perverse man, Talon." But she didn't waste any more time on the enigmatic warrior. She pushed into Griffon's study.

The room was big. The furnishings heavy. The atmosphere lonely and brooding as Griffon stood in front of the fireplace, staring down at the remains of a dead fire.

At the sound of her entrance he turned from his dark contemplation of the charred logs and cold, gray ashes. His eyes widened in surprise to see her standing there, then narrowed to irritated green bands. "Where's Talon?"

She tipped her head toward the door she'd closed behind her. "Just outside."

"Why didn't he radio ahead and tell me you were coming?"

"Because I told him if he did, I'd wring his neck."

Griffon's expression turned sardonic. "And that worried him?"

"The thought of me doing it in front of Perry did."

His gaze dropped to Perry. Sadness and longing flashed in his eyes. But he quickly smoothed his expression into his professional mask and raised his gaze to hers. "Is there something you need?"

Yes, I need you to tell me what demons are driving you. The words hovered on her lips. But she didn't say them. One look at his shuttered expression told her a frontal attack would be useless. She'd have to use a more subtle approach. She shook her head and glanced around the room, checking to see if it was baby safe. When she didn't see anything that would hurt Perry or that Perry might destroy, she set her down on the carpet. "I don't need anything. Perry and I just came to visit. I thought you might like to get to know your daughter a little more."

His eyes darted to Perry, who was busy crawling toward a bookcase on the far wall.

Juliana smiled. More books to toss around. When she looked back to Griffon she found him staring at Perry again, that sad, haunted look in his eyes.

But when he looked back to her, he'd once again masked the expression. "I'm sorry. You should have had Talon call. I could have told him I was too busy this morning to see you."

She gave him a skeptical look. "Too busy doing what? Staring into the fireplace?"

"I wasn't staring into the fireplace. I was deciding whether or not to accept a job."

"No you weren't, you—"

A sharp knock echoed through the room, the door burst open and two hurricanes—dressed like little girls—blew into the room.

"Hallie! Camilla! Wait!" An exasperated female voice came from a ways down the hall.

But it didn't stop the young girls. They flew into the room, straight to Griffon. "Uncle Griff, Uncle Griff! Look what I drew for you on the way down." The tallest of the girls thrust a piece of paper at Griffon. "Mama says I'm getting better every day. She says I'm going to be a great artist when I grow up."

Griffon held the picture up, studying it as he dropped his free hand around the girl's shoulders. "Well, I think she's right. This is a wonderful unicorn."

Juliana stood silently watching. Griffon smiled easily and his eyes twinkled as he talked to the small girls—one with long curly black hair that couldn't have been more than seven and the other about a year younger with short curly blond hair. No shadows clouded his eyes as they had when he'd watched Perry only moments before. It seemed that children in general didn't upset him. Just his own child put shadows in his eyes.

"You two little heathens, get back here." A blond woman, tall, thin and pretty, breezed into the room with the same energy the children had shown. "Sorry, Griff. I told them to wait."

He waved away her apology. "Don't worry, they're fine."

The woman noticed Juliana's presence. "Oh, dear, we're interrupting. I'm sorry." She turned back to Griffon. "Talon didn't say you had guests. Not that he had time as the little monsters charged past. We'll wait in the salon until you're finished." She put a hand on each girl in an attempt to disengage them from Griffon.

Griffon shook his head. "Don't go. I was just telling Juliana I'd have to speak to her later. That I was waiting for someone." He gave Juliana a pointed look.

The blonde shook her head. "Don't be silly. We can wait."

Juliana felt suddenly awkward and out of place—and hurt. Who was this beautiful woman and these two children that Griffon was obviously close to? "Griffon's right. I've obviously come at a bad time. We'll see him later." She tried to ignore the squeezing sensation in her chest as she strode to the bookshelves and scooped Perry into her arms.

Two high pitched squeals broke the silence. "A baby! Mama, look, a baby." The two girls broke away from Griffon and raced her way.

"Girls! Slow down."

The girls slowed just in time to keep from running into Juliana. "Can we see her?"

Juliana just wanted to leave. But she didn't want to be rude to the little girls. It wasn't their fault Griffon obviously adored them while he seemed determined to shun his own child. "Sure. But then we have to go." Her heart aching, she turned Perry in her arms so she was facing the little girls. "Her name is Perry."

"Sorry, Griff. The women in this family seem to be completely out of control."

Juliana looked up at the deep male voice. A man was just coming through the study door. He was using a cane to walk, but his shoulders were broad, and the muscles under his casual khakis and polo shirt hard. He exuded strength and vitality as he made his way to Griffon. A scar slashed across the left side of his face, but it didn't detract from his handsomeness. In fact, it added a dangerous, dashing quality that was very appealing.

The man's sharp gaze settled immediately on Juliana and Perry. "I'm sorry. We didn't know Griffon had company. We can wait."

Griffon shook his head again. "Juliana was just leaving."

"Don't be ridiculous, Griff," the blonde said. "There's no reason for her to leave. She and I can chat while you and Jason conduct your business. Now, introduce us all."

Juliana grimaced at Griffon's blatant attempt to get rid of her. But she didn't budge. Now that she knew the woman had a husband—the man with the cane had sidled up to her and dropped his arm familiarly, possessively around her waist—she wanted to know who these people were. What part they played in Griffon's life.

Griffon's forehead crinkled unhappily, but he made no further attempt to oust Juliana and Perry. He and the others joined her and the girls at the bookcases.

"Jason and Angie," Griffon began. "This is Juliana Bondevik and her daughter, Perry. Juliana, Jason and Angie Kent. And their two children, Hallie and Camilla." Griffon turned to Jason. "Juliana is the daughter to the chancellor of Bjorli."

Recognition flashed in Jason's eyes as he took Juliana's hand. "Ah, I know your father well. I worked for him a few times when I was part of Griffon's team. A pleasure to meet you."

So Jason had worked with Griffon. Good, the Kents probably knew Griffon well. With a little luck she just might learn something from Angie that would help her figure out Griffon's demons. Or something that might work as leverage to get him to open up.

Juliana took Jason's hand for a quick handshake. "Nice to meet you."

Jason studied Perry with a sharp, knowing eye. Then he turned that sharp gaze on her. "Beautiful baby."

Heat flushed Juliana's cheeks. He knew. But thankfully, he didn't seem inclined to comment. She tipped her head. "Thank you."

Angie gave Juliana a reassuring smile. "Let's go sit and talk while the boys get their business taken care of."

Juliana followed Angie and her children to the sofa, anxious to get on with their little chat. They all settled on the sofa. Perry in Juliana's lap and both girls doing a pretty respectable job of climbing into their mom's.

"We're adopted." The older girl, Hallie, piped up, flipping her long black curly hair away from her face. "I was adopted first. But Camilla was my best friend and we couldn't leave her at the home all alone, so we adopted her, too."

Juliana smiled at the energetic imp. "Is that so? Cool."

Both heads bobbed up and down enthusiastically. "Yeah, it's a lot cooler than being stuck in a group home," the younger girl said with a savvy look. "Mrs. Carmichael was nice. But it's a *lot* nicer having a mom and dad of our own. And we don't have to share *anything* now." The last was delivered in a conspiratorial whisper.

Juliana smiled. "Well, that's definitely a plus."

Angie laughed as she tickled both girls and then lifted them off her lap onto the floor. "Why don't you two go get your puzzles down and put a few of them together while Juliana and I talk? Okay?"

The girls nodded, scampered over to the bookcase and pulled out two puzzle boxes.

Juliana stared in amazement. Griff had toys in his study? She looked over to where Griffon stood with Jason, discussing their business. The man had toys in his study? Amazing. She turned back to Angie, more determined than ever to drag out everything the woman knew about Griffon. "So, have you known Griffon long?"

Angie tipped a shoulder. "I've known him a little over a year. But Jason worked for him for several years. They're very close."

Better and better.

But before she could ask her next question Angie tipped her head toward Perry. "Jason was right, she's a beautiful baby."

Juliana smiled. "Thank you. I'm pretty fond of her."

Angie touched Perry's hair. "She has your hair."

"Yes."

"And Griffon's eyes."

Heat stained Juliana's cheeks again, but she wasn't going to deny Perry's heritage. "Yes."

"Griffon never told us he had a child."

Juliana looked down at Perry, her fingers fussing with the her daughter's ruffled skirt. "He didn't know."

"Ah."

Perry cooed and pulled at Juliana's hair. The men's hushed voices sounded in the background as they discussed their business.

When some of the heat left Juliana's cheeks she forced herself to look back to Angie.

The woman raised a questioning brow. "How does he feel about the news?"

Juliana would probably have told anyone else it was none of their business. But there was nothing but compassion and concern in Angie's eyes. And shutting the woman out wouldn't get Juliana's questions about Griffon answered. "I don't know how he feels. The words that come out of his mouth don't seem to match what I see in his eyes."

Perry started to squirm in her lap, her gaze glued on Angie's girls as they played with the puzzles. Juliana put her on the floor and watched her crawl off to "help" the older girls.

She caught Griffon watching, too. His gaze tracked Perry's every move. And in that vigilant gaze Juliana saw again the painful longing she'd seen in his office. So *why* was he doing everything in his power to distance himself from his daughter?

"What are the words coming out of his mouth?" Angie's question broke into Juliana's thoughts.

"That I should take Perry back to Bjorli and tell her he's dead."

Angie gasped and glanced over her shoulder at Griffon. When she looked back, her brows were crumpled together in concern. "You're not going to do that, are you?"

"I'm not sure Griffon is going to give me a choice in the matter."

Angie hesitated, no doubt debating whether or not she should put herself in Juliana and Griffon's business, but evidently, her concern for the situation won out. "Listen, I don't know a lot about Griffon. But from what Jason has told me and from my own few encounters, I believe Griffon is a good man. An honorable man. I would have thought he was a loving man." She shook her head in confusion. "Why does he want you to tell Perry he's dead?"

Juliana worried a crease in her capri pants. How much did she want to confide in this woman? She'd met her only five minutes ago. And yet, the concern in her eyes seemed genuine. And right now Juliana could use a friend. "I don't know. He's alluded to some demons. But he won't tell me what they are."

"And you're going to let him get away with that?"

Juliana grimaced. "I'm having a little trouble pinning him down long enough to get any answers. And in this place, it's pretty easy for him to slip away."

"So take him somewhere else."

"If only it was that easy. But I don't believe he'd go anywhere else with me. And secondly, I'm not a guest here. Technically, I'm a prisoner."

Angie's eyes went wide. "How's that?"

Juliana shook her head. "It's a long, complicated story, but as far as Griffon is concerned I'm here because my father wanted me safe from the protests going on in my country."

Angie winced. "A definite problem. But there has to be a way around it."

A picture of the little cabin Juliana had seen the day she'd tried to go over the fence suddenly flashed in her mind. She looked over to Griffon. He and Jason had their heads bent together, their expressions serious as they talked. If she didn't do something drastic, he'd just elude her at every turn.

And she'd always wondered what it would be like to live in a little cabin in the woods.

She turned back to Angie with a conspiratorial smile. "Maybe there is a way."

Griff shook Jason's hand and gave Angie and the girls each a hug as they said their goodbyes at the study door. Normally he enjoyed their visits. But today, seeing Jason and Angie's love for each other, their love for their children, their happiness as a family was like having acid poured in an open wound. He needed them gone.

He watched Juliana shake Jason's hand.

She was so beautiful.

She had on the same outfit she'd worn to the gym the other day. Black, skintight pants that ended halfway between her knees and ankles. Pants that made his pulse throb and his fingers itch. And the short top that left an inch or two of soft skin showing above her waistband wasn't helping a bit to slow the need racing through his blood.

And the tiny baby she held in her arms was twisting his heart into a thousand knots.

He needed to get Jason and his family, the perfect example of just what he would be giving up when he sent Juliana and Perry home, out of his house. And then he needed to get Juliana and Perry back to their room before he made another stupid, impossible decision like the one he'd made while sitting against that tree in the woods the other day.

He watched as Juliana gave Angie a hug. When Angie stepped back, the two women exchanged a look—one of those looks one woman gives another when a silent understanding has passed between them—and then the Kents left.

Griff closed the door behind them and turned to Juliana. "What were you two ladies talking about?"

Juliana gave a practiced shrug. "Just women stuff. Nothing that would interest you."

He wouldn't bet on that. He didn't like the calculating look in those blue, Nordic eyes one bit.

Juliana shifted Perry in her arms, tugging the ruffled purple and white hem over chubby knees. "What did Jason want?"

Griff stepped back, putting some distance between them. Being close enough to smell her soft, sweet perfume was scrambling his brain. "Apparently there are four children trapped in a orphanage in Bosnia, and troops are closing in." He grimaced. "And some fool-hearted senator's daughter has gone to get them. Jason wants me to send a man to make sure everyone gets out in one piece."

She raised a brow. "And?"

"And what?"

"You're sending someone aren't you?"

Griff thought of Matt's desertion when Perry arrived on the scene. It was definitely time for the giant soldier to get on with his life. "Oh, yeah, I'm sending someone."

"Good. Now, I need to talk to you."

His gut tightened. "I thought you just came down to visit?"

"Well, that was twenty minutes ago. Life changes."

And he was pretty damned sure he wasn't going to like the change. But he forced himself to ask, anyway. "What do you need?"

"I've decided you're right, after all. I don't think it's good for Perry to be here in the mansion. It's too much of a military environment. I want to take her to the cabin while we're here."

His brows crashed together. "What cabin?"

"That little one by the stream at the back of the compound."

"Don't be ridiculous. That thing's over a hundred years old. There's no electricity or running water."

She shrugged. "I don't care."

Well he damned well did. He'd grown up in abject poverty. Grown up in a broken-down trailer where electricity and running water depended on his father's erratic habit of paying the bills. Where even when the bills were paid, the stench of poverty tainted every piece of his life. And he'd hated it.

He scowled. "You're not keeping my daughter in that broken-down old shack."

She scowled right back. "Griffon, you want me to tell her you're dead, how can you possibly care where I keep her?"

"I care," he growled.

But his show of temper didn't impress Juliana. She just lifted that stubborn chin. "Then prove it. You said yourself this wasn't a healthy environment for a kid. And despite the fact the cabin is small and needs to be cleaned before we can move in, it's quaint and quiet and peaceful. I want you to move us there. And I want *you* to guard us while we're there. Not Matt or Talon or Marshall. You."

The tightness in his gut turned into a hard knot. Now they were getting to the heart of her argument. He narrowed his eyes. "You're not worried about the environment here. Nor do you care how peaceful it is at that cabin. You just want to get me in a place where you can corner me and harry me to death with your questions."

She shrugged. "So? You're a tough guy. Big, bad soldier. Surely you're not afraid your defenses won't hold out against a mere woman and a twelve-month-old baby when my ammunition is something as benign as *questions*."

Afraid? He was scared to death. There was nothing "mere" about either of them. He wanted Juliana so badly, his teeth ached. Wanted to feel the soft silkiness of her skin against his. Wanted to taste the rich warmth of her mouth. Wanted to hear her gentle laughter in the dark of the night. And the tiny baby in her arms...

God, his heart bled just looking at her. Being stuck in a tiny cabin with both of them would be slow, agonizing torture. And it would be dangerous.

He was hanging on to his resolve to send them both away, to never see either of them again, by the barest of threads. Sticking himself where they would become even closer to his heart would be a foolish risk. For all of them.

Juliana cocked her head, studying him. Her lips suddenly pressed into a narrow line as if something unpleasant had just occurred to her. "Listen, if you're worried that I'm after you—that I'll try to rekindle what we had in the Alps—don't. You walked away from me when you didn't know who I was. Now, even if you made overtures, I'd wonder if what you really wanted was me or the power that being with me would give you."

Despite the fact he knew she had every right to do so, he hated that she thought he'd stoop so low. He huffed in irritation. "Don't you think if that was in my mind I would have already made overtures to you?"

She shrugged. "I don't know. All I know is I've already been one man's attempted path to power. I won't be another's."

Griff stilled. "What man?"

She grimaced at her own words. "Never mind."

"I don't want to never mind. I want to hear the story." He tried to keep the possessive note out of his voice. He sure as hell had no right to it. But it was there, as loud as artillery in the dead of night.

She shot him a disparaging look. "The ruffling of feathers is a bit hypocritical, don't you think? For a man who couldn't manage a civil goodbye?"

Hypocritical or not, he wanted an answer. And he was happy to wait for one. He crossed his arms over his chest and rocked back on his heels.

"You can stand there all day, Griffon, and I'm not going to answer you. Suffice it to say that when you're the chancellor's daughter people view you as a commodity. You're not a person, you're a way for them to get closer to the chancellor of Bjorli—or the crown of Bjorli. You're a way for them to get what they want out of life. The one chance I had at believing someone loved me, just me, not the chancellor's daughter, was with you. And we both know how that turned out, don't we?"

Guilt slashed at him. He'd never considered there would be hazards to being born rich or being born to a high political standing. But he knew how the world worked. Now that she'd pointed it out, he could easily see how men might try to take advantage of a woman in her position.

It probably happened all the time. And she'd just told him it had happened to her. And while he hated the thought of her with another man on a purely male level, he hated more that some bastard had used her. It was like a knife in the heart to know he had added to her pain. That he'd made her think—just as some other bastard had—that he had used her.

He met her gaze head-on, determined to convince her that his feelings for her had been real. "I didn't use you in Switzerland, Juliana. If you hadn't been there with your beautiful smile and your gentle conversation, no other woman would have been in my bed. I guarantee it."

Her eyes seemed to mist and something flashed there—hope, maybe—but she blinked hard and when she opened her eyes again there was nothing but determination in them. "If those feelings were real, if you really cared for me, if you're really sorry for the way you left, then you owe me, Griffon. And this is what I'm asking for. Six days of your time. From now until the end of the protests when you can put me back on a plane and send me home, I want you to spend time with me and your daughter at that cabin. And if you think you don't owe it to me, surely you realize you owe it to your daughter."

"I seriously doubt Perry cares if she spends any time in a drafty old cabin. And even if I give her those six days, she'll never know she had them."

Her gaze bore into his. "She'll know, Griffon. If you really spend time *with* her, playing with her, talking with her, instead of just staying with us in the cabin, she'll know. Deep in her heart, deep in her soul, she'll know that at one point in her life her father cared for her." She snuggled the baby against her breast. "She deserves that, Griffon. It's a fair request."

There wasn't a damned fair thing about any of this. For any of them. And every survival instinct in his body told him to hand mother and daughter over to Talon and demand that neither of them be allowed to leave their bedroom until it was time for them to get on their plane. But he couldn't do it.

Damn him to hell, he couldn't do it. The one good thing he'd had from his childhood had been his mother's love. He'd lost her when he was young, but her love had gotten him through more than one dark, hellish night.

Not that he believed Perry would have a life anything like his. The whole reason he was sending them away was to make sure she didn't. But still...

If Juliana was right, if he could somehow impart even a tiny bit of the love he felt for that little girl—without putting her in any danger—it would be worth whatever torture he went through.

And...before Juliana left here, he wanted her to know that at one time in her life *she'd* been cherished. Not for what she could do for someone's career. But for herself. He didn't know how he was going to do it and still keep the distance he would need to put them on that plane next week. But he'd find a way. Juliana was right, he owed her.

He nodded. "All right, we'll stay at the cabin. But I'm not answering your questions, Juliana. I'm doing this for Perry." *And for you.* "And don't get your hopes up for it happening today, or even tomorrow. I wasn't kidding when I said I wouldn't have my daughter staying in a rat trap. It'll take a day or two to get it ready. Until then I want you to stay in your room and quit using Perry as a free pass to wander at will."

Chapter Ten

Griff sat in the Jeep with Juliana and Perry riding in the seat next to him, the morning sun still low in the sky. It had taken two days for him to get the cabin to an acceptable point.

It had taken his men a full day to clean a hundred years of dirt from the walls and floors before they could start moving furniture and amenities in. And they'd spent all day yesterday with those details.

Juliana hadn't been happy about the delay. An opinion she'd shared with Talon numerous times over the small time span, if the soldier's reports had meant anything. And one she'd shared with Griff first thing this morning. But the delay had been unavoidable.

Juliana had been raised in the Bjorlian palace, there was no way he was going to have her staying in a ramshackle cabin. And he wasn't going to have Perry crawling around on cold drafty floors, either.

The Jeep's engine whined in his ears and the cool morning air nipped at his face. The cabin might be ready to go, but he sure as hell wasn't. He'd rather be walking into battle right now than heading to that tiny cabin. His nerves were drawn tighter than a hangman's noose. What had he been thinking when he'd agreed to this ridiculous plan? That cabin was tiny, and it had grown tinier with every stick of furniture he'd stuck in it. They weren't going to be able to move without bumping into each other.

He knew how tight quarters could grate on people's nerves and bring emotions to a boiling point. He'd seen the ugly results time and time again inside the trailer he'd grown up in.

He couldn't let that happen here.

He drew a deep breath, flexed his hands on the wheel and then slowly released the air from his lungs, trying to slow the racing of his heart and get ahold of the dark tendrils wrapping around his neck and squeezing hard. This situation was nothing like his childhood. Nothing bad was going to happen in this cabin.

He glanced at Juliana. She sat in the seat next to him, Perry in her arms, the wind blowing her silky hair behind her, her cheeks rosy from the morning chill. She was so beautiful. He couldn't imagine hurting her.

But how could he be certain he wouldn't? Surely his father had loved his mother once. He couldn't imagine his mother marrying the man if he'd abused her before the wedding. So when had the old man started hitting her? A year after the wedding? A month? A week? Oh, God, what had he gotten himself into?

He took another deep breath, forcing those thoughts into a dark closet and slamming the door on them. He was being ridiculous. This little interlude would last only four days. He could certainly keep things together for that length of time.

He maneuvered the Jeep through the woods and pulled up in front of the cabin. He vaulted out and strode around to Juliana's side. Taking her hand, he helped her out. "I'll take you inside and then I'll come back out for the bags."

"Sounds good." When they rounded the front of the Jeep, she stopped, undoubtedly taking in the changes in the place since the last time she'd been here.

The blackened logs making up the cabin's walls looked the same, of course, but the porch was swept and the windows were no longer opaque with dirt and grime. Their soft ripples sparkled in the sunshine now. And he'd had one of the men mow a small lawn around the place.

She hefted Perry to her other arm and looked to him with a huge grin. "Isn't it beautiful?"

He'd left this place intact because he had a certain respect for its perseverance. Anything that could make it through a hundred years of hard times had a right to go on existing. But only someone who hadn't spent their life in a place just as run-down would see it as beautiful. He gave her a skeptical look and shook his head. "Quaint, maybe. In a dilapidated sort of way."

She chuckled softly, totally unaffected by his cynicism. "Come on, let's go in. I want to see what your industrious soldiers have spent the last two days doing to the place."

He jogged ahead of her so he could get the door. Pushing it open, he stepped aside and waved her in. He held his breath as she stepped by him into the house. He wanted her to like it.

Which was damned ridiculous. This had been her idea, not his. As long as she was comfortable he shouldn't care if she liked the place's new look or not. But still...

He followed her in, taking in her expression.

She looked around the cabin's main room—a small living room-kitchen combination. Her eyes went wide and a burst of laughter fell from her lips. But seeing him watching her with such expectation, she quickly squelched it, clamping a hand over her mouth.

Disappointment slid through him. "You don't like it."

Her eyes went wider as she realized he'd wanted to please her. She quickly smoothed all the humor from her features and lowered her hand. "No, I love it," she said, doing her best to convince him she did.

He scowled at her. "No you don't. You hate it."

Her sincere expression crumpled and another laugh slipped from her lips, but this one was softer, gentler. A laugh meant to include him, not poke fun at him. "No, I don't hate it. It's just that...it's a *cabin*, Griffon. You don't think oriental, *silk* rugs and grand furniture are a little much?''

He took in the room, the noose tightening around his neck a little more. He wasn't getting off on the right foot here. ''I had my men bring the softest rugs from the mansion because I wanted Perry crawling around on something comfortable. And I brought the best furniture because I thought you'd like it.''

Her expression softened and she smiled. ''I do like it. It's beautiful. And not because you brought the fancy furniture, but because you put so much thought and care into it.'' She laid her hand on his arm. ''Thank you.''

Heat poured through him. He'd dreamed about her touch for the past two years. And it was every bit as soft and exhilarating as he remembered. Great. Just what he needed. A little sexual tension to add to the already mounting tension building inside him.

He stepped away from her. At least she appreciated him trying to make her and the baby comfortable. ''There were some things I couldn't make better. There's no electricity. After sundown we'll have to use kerosene lamps.''

She just smiled. ''Doing without some of today's modern conveniences is half the charm.''

He just barely managed not to roll his eyes. Only someone who had never done without would think so. ''Yeah, well—'' He tipped his head toward the back of the cabin. ''The latrine's out back.''

''Latrine?''

''No running water, remember?''

A light pink tinged her cheeks, and she wrinkled her nose. "Oh, yeah."

She didn't look quite as thrilled with the loss of that convenience. Maybe this was his out. "Just say the words, Juliana, and I'll have you back in the mansion in a heartbeat." Back to the mansion where we'll all be safe.

She shook her head. "Don't be ridiculous. I did summer camps as a kid. This isn't the first outhouse I've used."

"Good for you." He couldn't quite keep the sarcasm from his voice or the dread from filling his chest. "I'm going to get the bags." He left the cabin, pulling giant breaths of fresh air into his lung as he made his way to the Jeep.

Once there he leaned against the front fender, closed his eyes and tried not to think of the electricity still surging through his body. Ridiculous. He wasn't some sex-starved teenager who lost his mind over a single, innocent touch. He was a grown man.

Except, right now he felt like a sex-starved teenager.

It was going to be a long, torturous four days. And he might as well get on with it. He pulled in a breath and pushed away from the Jeep. Grabbing the bags, he headed back into the cabin. When he got there, Juliana was standing in the open doorway that led to the cabin's other room. The room he'd had his men move a dresser...and queen-size bed into.

She looked back at him, a slight flush washing over her cheeks.

Was she thinking of the time they'd shared a bed?

Or was she wondering if he wanted to share this one? He needed to put an end to that thought. For both of them. He set her bags and his duffle down on the floor. "You'll—" His voice was conspicuously rough. He cleared his throat and tried again. "You'll sleep in there, of course. I'll bunk out here on the sofa."

She looked away, the pink tinge in her cheeks turning a little redder. "Okay. Sounds good." But her voice didn't sound good, it sounded…embarrassed? Sad? He thought her expression might tell him more, but when she looked back to him, it was an unreadable mask. "I think I'll unpack. Would you mind watching Perry while I do it?" She smiled ruefully. "She has this thing about suitcases."

He lifted a brow in question.

"She likes to take everything out and throw it around."

"Ah, I see the problem." But he hadn't realized until this moment how much of a problem he had. He stared at the small bundle of smiles and mischief in Juliana's arms. Promising to spend time with her was one thing. Actually doing it was quite another. A thousand fears poured into his head.

Fear that he'd hurt her.

Fear that he'd fall in love with her and not want to let her go.

But he couldn't very well turn Juliana down. He'd promised he'd do more than be a presence in the house. He'd promised to spend time *with* his baby. "Sure, leave her out here. I'll…watch her."

Juliana shot him a reassuring smile and set Perry

down on the floor. "Thanks. It won't take long." She strode over to him, grabbed her bags and headed back to the bedroom.

Oh, geez, he'd been so caught up wondering how he was going to resist Perry's charms he'd totally forgotten his manners. He strode after her, reaching for the bags. "I'll get those."

"Don't be silly, Griffon. I'm not helpless. Watch the baby." She disappeared into the bedroom, closing the door behind her. And leaving him and Perry... alone.

He stared at the child crawling around the floor, exploring. She was so small. Tiny really. And fragile. So, so fragile. His mouth went dry. A cold sweat coated his palms. He didn't belong anywhere near anything that tiny or innocent or breakable. Even if he had made some insane promise.

He carefully walked around his tiny daughter and sat down on the sofa. He could watch her from here. Make sure she didn't get into anything that would hurt her. But beyond that he wasn't budging from his spot.

He watched her, marveling at her. With her petite, upturned nose and her delicate, bow-shaped mouth she reminded him of one of his sister's dolls. Or one of the fairies from the stories his mother had told. God, she was cute.

He smiled as she crawled over to his duffle and checked it out, pulling at the straps, trying to work the zipper. When it didn't budge, she lost interest and headed in the other direction to check out the rest of the living room. Her travels eventually brought her to the open fireplace. She took one look at the small space created by the stone walls and crawled right in.

He sat forward on the sofa. "Perry, come away from there. It's dirty." It wasn't, of course. The fireplace was as clean as the rest of the cabin. But it was a fireplace. Children didn't belong inside fireplaces, even when they weren't in use.

Perry looked at him and smiled, a big toothy grin. But she didn't move.

He gritted his teeth. He didn't want to go get her. When he'd promised Juliana he would spend time with his daughter he'd known it would involve holding the child, touching her. But now he didn't think that was a good idea. His hands had been used for nothing but warfare for the past seventeen years. Best if he kept them away from Perry entirely.

It was an irrational thought. He'd held children on the battlefield without hurting them. He'd held Perry in his office without hurting her. But here in this cabin ugly memories pounded in his head like African war drums. Memories of his father's ugly temper, his uncontrollable rages and his hard, punishing fists. With this place closing in on him like a bad dream and that noose tightening relentlessly around his neck, he didn't want his hands anywhere near Perry.

"Come on, Sweetie, get out of there. Come over here and you can throw the clothes out of my bag." He leaned down, unzipped his duffle and pulled the sides open, enticing Perry out of the stone cubby.

She gurgled something that must have translated into "You can't bribe me" because she turned her back on him and crawled a little farther into the fire-place.

"Perry," he growled, trying a more threatening tone.

But his daughter wasn't impressed. She just laughed and babbled and slapped the stone floor of the fire pit. And then stuck her fingers in her mouth.

That was it. Drums pounding in his head or not, he had to get her out of that fireplace. He pushed up from the sofa and strode over to the brick chimney. Ignoring the cold sweat prickling his skin, he picked up the tot and—holding her as far from his body as he could get her—he carried her back to the sofa and set her down by his duffle.

She hit the floor running—or crawling as the case might be—and headed right back to the fireplace.

Frustration and fear poured through him. This was exactly the type of situation that would result in violence when he was a kid. Someone would ignore their father's dictates and all hell would break out. He wasn't going to let that happen here. "*Juliana,*" he hollered.

Juliana's door opened. "What's up."

"You're going to have to take care of Perry. She wants to play in the fireplace, and I can't get her to stop."

She looked at the stone fireplace. "So let her play in it."

Had she lost her mind? "I'm not letting her play in there. It's a *fireplace.*"

She shrugged. "There's no fire in it. And it's clean."

"Not that clean. And she's putting her fingers in her mouth."

"Griffon. I know you're not used to being around a child, let alone your own. But you need to relax a bit. A little dirt isn't going to hurt her."

Relax? He couldn't relax. This whole setup was going to blow up in his face. "This isn't going to work. I'm a soldier not a baby-sitter. I shouldn't be looking after her. What if I hurt her?"

Juliana's brows snapped together. "You're not going to hurt her."

"What makes you think that? Do you *know* what I do for a living? Do you have any idea what being a mercenary *means?*" Do you have any idea at all of the violence I'm capable of?

Concern furrowed her forehead and she strode toward him, her hand held out in supplication. "Griffon. Being a mercenary doesn't make you an unfit parent."

Maybe. Maybe not. But there were other things in his past that sure as hell did. The noose around his neck tightened until he couldn't breathe. He wasn't going to make it through one day. How the hell would he make it through four? He backed away from Juliana, shaking his head and holding his hand up to forestall her. "I've got to get out of here." Without another word he strode out of the cabin.

Juliana watched Griffon dash out the door, his words echoing through her head.

I'm a soldier, not a babysitter. I shouldn't be looking after her. What if I hurt her?

The old women - and - children - don't - belong - anywhere - near - military - installations - and - their - men story again. At least the man was consistent. But was he being honest? She hadn't thought so when he'd explained he'd left her in Switzerland because he hadn't wanted to bring her here, to a soldier's stronghold, a place where war was practiced. But what about now?

She thought about the haunted look in his eyes. The desperation in his voice. He was afraid of hurting Perry. No doubt about it. But was it because he was a soldier? Or did this, too, have to do with his demons?

She stared at the door the irritating man had just slammed out of and sighed in frustration. She'd brought Griffon to this cabin because she thought he'd be easier to pin down. But even here he'd managed to slip away.

So now what?

She strode to the sofa, slumped down into its leather folds and watched Perry sitting in the fireplace on her ruffle-clad bottom.

While Juliana wanted to get to the source of Griffon's demons, there was another, more immediate issue on the table she needed to address. Did she believe Griffon was capable of hurting his daughter, the precious little girl sitting in the fireplace, cooing and babbling and listening to her voice echo in the small, enclosed chamber?

Juliana thought about the two weeks she'd spent with Griffon at the lodge. Thought of the way he'd always been there to help her up after a spill on the slopes. Thought of the way he'd held doors open for her and brought drinks for her and made sure she'd had every comfort. Thought of his eager but gentle touch when the lights went out. Thought of the reverent way he'd run his fingers over Perry's hair in his office.

She didn't know who Griffon Tyner was on the battlefield. She didn't know what demons nipped at the man's heels. But she did know, deep down in her heart, without a flicker of doubt, he wasn't capable of hurting his daughter.

And if he thought she was going to coddle him, let him wallow in his fears by keeping his daughter safely out of his circle, he was so, *so* wrong.

But she'd give him a little breathing space. For now. At least where his daughter was concerned. But as far as his demons went... As soon as she put Cinderella down for her nap, she was going soldier hunting.

She gave Perry a wicked smile. "And then, sweetie pie, your poor, poor daddy will have no escape."

Chapter Eleven

Perry was finally down for her afternoon nap. She'd played hard all morning, cooing into the chimney and unpacking Griffon's bag for him. Juliana smiled, looking at the clothes strewn around the living room floor. She'd thought briefly about rezipping the bag and putting it out of Perry's reach, but then she'd come to her senses.

She wasn't the one who'd stormed out of the house and left her bag open on the floor. He had. And he could clean up the mess when he came back. But she had kindly bothered to make him lunch. And now she was going to find the stubborn man and feed it to him. Along with a few choice questions.

She grabbed the plate of bologna sandwiches and two glasses of iced tea. Making her way through the living room, she stepped over his shaving kit and around a pair of plain white briefs. Desire slid through her. She remembered—vividly—how he looked in nothing but his briefs. His strong shoulders and washboard stomach above the white expanse, the long, strong muscles of his thighs below and the soft white cotton cupping the more-than-generous bulge of his manhood.

Another wave of tingling heat hit her. Lord help her. She shoved the erotic and *totally* unproductive thought aside. She wasn't here to titillate her dormant sexuality. She was here to decide if she wanted Griffon in his daughter's life. And to do that she needed answers. Forcing her mind back to the task at hand, she strode out of the cabin and onto the porch.

She looked around, wondering if she'd find him near or far. She'd peeked out the window a few times since he'd left, looking for him. But she'd seen nothing but the woods. She saw him now, though. He was sitting on the ground, leaning against the side of the Jeep, watching her.

She strode over and stood above him, giving the Jeep and ground a baleful look. "Gee, this looks comfy."

"More comfortable than a lot of seats I've had over the years, believe me."

Yes, as a soldier he would have sat in much less comfortable spots. But right now the last thing she wanted to talk about was his soldiering. She felt positive he was using his profession as a smoke screen to hide his real demons. And with only four days left she didn't have time for the game. She hefted the fare in her hands. "I brought you lunch."

"Thank you, but I'm not hungry."

She flashed him a steely smile. "Well, I made it, and you, sir, are going to eat it. Hungry or not." She waved the plate toward the cabin. "Do you want to sit on the porch or go inside? It's pretty hot out here."

He looked at the cabin as though it was the devil incarnate. "No, I'm comfortable here."

She sighed in resignation. "All righty, then, this is the spot." She shoved the plate and glass into his hands and lowered herself beside him, the ice in her own glass chinking softly as the tea sloshed.

He gave her a dark scowl as she settled on the ground next to him.

But she ignored it, took a cooling sip of her tea and then got down to business. "Want to tell me what happened this morning?"

He looked away. "Nothing happened this morning."

She wrinkled her nose. "I'll take that as a no." She watched him stare darkly at the cabin, wishing she knew what was going on in his head. Wishing she had the key to open up his mind and look inside.

He ignored her scrutiny, for a while, but then he turned to her with an impatient glance. "What?"

She met his irritated gaze squarely. "I'm wondering why you're so tense and why you're looking at that cabin as if it was going to get up and bite you."

He opened his mouth to protest, but before he could get a sound out, she held up her hand to forestall him. "Don't snap at me again. You agreed to come to this cabin and spend time with your daughter. And sitting out here by this Jeep doesn't qualify."

Guilt flashed in his eyes and he looked away, his gaze once again settling on the cabin. For a full minute silence reigned. Then he heaved a resigned sigh. "Maybe I am wondering if that cabin is going to bite me in the ass."

"How's that?"

He shook his head. "It's too small. I feel like I can't breathe in there."

She took in the tension at the corners of his eyes, the corners of his mouth. "I didn't know you were claustrophobic."

His lips formed a wry smile. "I'm not."

She sat quietly, waiting for him to go on. When he didn't, she tried to reassure him. "The cabin isn't that small, and there are only three of us it in. When it was built people raised households of ten or more in houses that size."

He ran a hand down his troubled face. "They still do."

She stilled. Was he alluding to modern families in general or to a very specific family? "Did your parents?" she asked carefully.

"Well, there weren't ten of us, thank God. And our house—our *trailer*—was a little bigger. But it didn't feel bigger. It was small and cramped and oppressive."

"You were poor." She couldn't quite keep the surprise from her voice.

"Very."

Sudden realization hit her. "That's why you bought the mansion for Freedom Rings. Not only because it was in a remote place, but because the mansion was confirmation you'd made it.''

"I suppose." His expression seemed remote as he stared at the cabin.

"But if you've left that poverty behind, and you clearly have, why does the cabin bother you so much?''

A muscle flexed along his jaw as he stared at the cabin. But he didn't answer her question.

She watched the dark shadows flit in his eyes. Obviously there was more bothering him than the size of the cabin or his past poverty. The third word he'd used to describe the trailer echoed in her head.

Oppressive.

"What was so horrible about living in that trailer that you're letting it ruin this time with your daughter?''

His expression hardened. "Leave it alone, Juliana.''

But she couldn't leave it alone. Perry's future depended on getting the answer. She huffed in frustration. "You know, Griffon, we've slept together, had a baby together, but I know virtually nothing about you, and—"

"You don't need to know anything about me. After these next four days, you'll never see me again.''

She narrowed her eyes. "I haven't decided that yet. So humor me. Tell me something about yourself. One thing," she demanded.

The sun beat down on them. The muscle along Griffon's jaw resumed its methodical tick.

She wanted to kick his stubborn hide, but a less

aggressive tack would probably get her further. She searched for a safe topic. One so benign he'd answer it just to get her off his back. "How many brothers and sisters did you have?"

He gave her a hard look from the corner of his eye. "You're not going to give up, are you?"

She shook her head. "No way. Instead of spending time with Perry this morning you ran out on her. So now I figure you owe me one. At least one. How many brothers and sisters did you have?"

Guilt once again flashed in his eyes when she mentioned Perry. He sighed in resignation. "There are four of us."

She breathed a tiny, tiny sigh of relief. It wasn't much, but it was a start. "How many boys and how many girls?"

"Two of each."

"What are their names?" She held her breath, hoping he'd continue to answer her questions.

His gaze took on a faraway look. As if he were looking into the past. "Annie. And Melissa. And Sean." His voice was quiet, subdued. Sad.

"Who's the oldest?" she asked gently.

Dark shadows filled his eyes. "I am."

Her heart clenched. What had put those shadows there? As the oldest, had he felt responsible for his brother and sisters. Had something bad happened? "Tell me about them. Are they—"

"Move on to something else, Juliana."

She wanted to push him harder. There was something here, something important. But she feared if she pushed too hard, he'd get up and walk away. She searched for another neutral question. "Tell me about your mother."

His expression softened, and the barest hint of a smile turned his lips. "She was beautiful. And sweet." He closed his eyes as if savoring a particularly precious memory. "And she loved her children."

Her heart stopped, and a hard lump formed in her throat. Whether it was his tone or the sad, wistful look on his face, she knew, without a doubt, that Griffon Tyner's mother had been the only person to show Griffon love. Her heart twisted. What had happened to his family?

She swallowed hard, fearing the answer to the next question, but she pushed it past her lips, anyway. "Is your mother still alive?"

He shook his head. "She died when I was eight."

Dear Lord. Eight. He'd barely had a chance to experience love when it had been snatched away. No wonder she'd seen such loneliness in his eyes at the lodge. A lump formed in her throat, and tears threatened to spill over her lashes.

But she quickly blinked them back. He wouldn't appreciate them, and they wouldn't help her get answers to her questions. And there were hundreds of questions swimming in her head.

She chose one. "What was your father like? Was he supportive after your mother died?"

The shadows in his eyes turned into thunderclouds, black and stormy. The tension in his face hardened. "The walk down memory lane is over, Juliana. Move on to something else or go back to your precious cabin.''

She flinched. He definitely had bad feelings about his dad. Which meant it was probably a subject she should explore further. But she was afraid if she tried to do it now, he'd clam up on her. So she'd move on to another subject. For now.

She shifted her gaze back to the cabin. ''Okay, let's talk about houses. Homes. Obviously, you're not comfortable in the cabin. And it goes without saying you didn't like the trailer you grew up in, but are you *happier* in your mansion? I admit you seem at ease within its walls, but...it seems an awfully lonely place.'' You seem awfully lonely there.

He shrugged. ''Being raised in a palace where your every need has been met, you probably place a much higher importance on happiness than the less fortunate of the world. Speaking from experience I can tell you that being comfortable isn't anything to sneeze at.''

Perhaps. But she had the distinct impression he'd be just as comfortable in a dry tent. And why not? Since his mother's death Juliana didn't think anyone had tried to make a home for him. From the way he'd reacted when she'd mentioned his dad, his father certainly never had. And if his mansion was any indication, Griffon didn't have a clue how to go about it himself.

His mansion was full of fancy furniture and pretty baubles, but it was lacking all the things that made a house a home. Family. Companionship. Love.

Juliana narrowed her gaze on the small heart-shaped window in the cabin's door. This cabin had known love. That's one reason why she'd wanted to come here. She'd wanted to share the simple intimacy the pioneer family had shared. Now she wanted something else. She wanted Griffon Tyner to feel again what a real home was.

But how was she going to do that in four short days? How would she do it at all, if Griffon wouldn't even come into the place?

Griffon leaned against the Jeep, the hot metal warming his back as he watched Juliana take a sip of her tea. She snuggled back against the Jeep, making herself more comfortable, a pensive look on her face. For the next few minutes she merely sat and nursed her icy drink.

He gave her a wry look. "Have you finally run out of questions?"

Her lips quirked. "For now."

"Well then, would you like a sandwich?" He held the plate out to her. He'd run out of the house because the cramped quarters had brought old memories back with frightening clarity. But it was too quiet out here, too hard to chase those memories away with nothing to occupy his thoughts. And he had a few questions of his own he wanted to ask.

Juliana would be gone in four days. Once he put her on that plane, he wouldn't interfere in her life again. And despite her protestations otherwise he wouldn't let her interfere in his life, either. But he wanted to make sure she and the baby would be okay.

He wanted to make sure they would have everything they needed.

Juliana gave him a rueful look and took one of the sandwiches from the plate. "I guess one of us should eat them."

He picked up the other one and took a hearty bite. In the wide expanse of the great outdoors and with Juliana's questions behind him, he was suddenly hungry. He took another bite of the bread and meat, followed it with a long swig of tea and listened to a songbird perched in a nearby tree.

The sandwich was good. The tea cool. The company perfect.

It was a quiet moment out of time. Peaceful and unencumbered and, sadly, temporary. But nothing lasted forever. Certainly not the good things in life. He intended to enjoy this moment while it lasted.

They ate in silent companionship, both lost in their own thoughts. He popped the last bite of sandwich into his mouth and swallowed it with a swig of tea. "I take it Perry's asleep."

Juliana nodded. "Yep. She's a good napper. She'll be down another hour or two."

"So tell me what it's like to be the chancellor's daughter."

She rolled her eyes. "You couldn't think of a more interesting topic than that?"

He could point out his question was a whole lot more interesting than talking about run-down trailers, but the last thing he wanted to do was get her back on that jag. So he settled for a more neutral prompt.

"It's interesting to me. What does the chancellor's daughter do all day?"

She gave him a disparaging look. "Mostly I watch after your daughter."

"What did you do *before* she was born?"

She shrugged. "The usual. I was on the board of a lot of charities. And the chancellor's family is forever attending one political function or another. It's a busy life, actually."

Busy, yes, but he didn't hear enough passion in her voice to think she found it overly rewarding. "Did you give up all charities and functions when Perry was born?"

"I kept my favorite charities, and there are certain political functions I can't avoid. But I slowed my schedule way down. Perry is so much more fun than dressing for effect."

He raised a brow. "I thought women liked dressing for effect."

"Not me. I hate the functions that require getting all decked out. The designers want me to spend hours poring through their creations, and then it takes hours to get ready. It drives me crazy. I'm definitely more a denim-and-cotton kind of gal."

He glanced down at the jeans covering her long, curvy legs. "Now that I think about it, I've never seen you in anything but jeans and snow pants." Desire shot through him. "Well, and those tight, short pants you wore the other day."

She chuckled softly. "You like those, huh?"

He shook his head. "'Fraid so. But I like pretty dresses, too."

"Boy, would you love the contents of my suitcase. It's loaded with all kinds of pretty dresses. But don't get your hopes up for seeing me in one. Not only do I not like dressing up, my goal is to go home without ever having worn one of them. That ought to get my dad's goat."

He thought about coaxing her into one of the dresses. He'd love to see her in something soft and feminine. But more stimulation was the last thing his libido needed. So he moved on to the questions he really wanted answered. "Okay, we'll consider having to dress for effect one of the hard parts of being the chancellor's daughter. Tell me about the others."

She shot him another one of those disparaging looks. "We're not going down that path, Griffon."

"What? Is this a one-sided conversation? You get to ask all the questions, and I just sit here like a dunce? It's my turn. Tell me about the downside of being the chancellor's daughter."

"I already did. Remember? People using me to get close to the chancellor or the king. You haven't forgotten. You just want details."

"Is it a crime to want to know about the life of the mother of my baby? Is it a crime to want to know what challenges my child might face?"

She gave a little sigh of defeat. "People using me is just part of the job, Griffon. The ugly part, yes. But I'm used to it."

"Maybe. But it still makes you sad."

"Yeah, well, we all have things that make us sad, don't we?"

Touché. But right now they were talking about her.

"Surely there must be someone who isn't interested in your connections. Someone who just likes to laugh and share time with you."

She shook her head.

He sighed in frustration. He didn't like the idea of sending her back to a place where she had no friends. Being a single parent had to be hard. He remembered how his mother had fought to keep things together after his father had cut her off from family and friends. Life had simply overwhelmed her.

Granted, his mother had an abusive husband to deal with, something Juliana wouldn't have. But still, life was difficult. A woman needed friends. He was hoping Juliana had someone besides her mother and father. Someone she'd simply overlooked. "What about the princess of Bjorli? She wouldn't have anything to gain from you, and she's about your age, isn't she?"

Juliana smiled, a little sadly. "Yes. And we were great friends once. But since she was kidnapped, she's become reclusive. She hardly leaves her room anymore. And she doesn't like people to visit, either."

He'd heard of the princess's kidnapping. It had been a two-week ordeal that had luckily ended in the Bjorlian Guard locating the kidnappers and storming their hideaway to get the girl back. Apparently, those two weeks had affected the princess deeply. "I'm sorry to hear that."

"So am I, and not just for me. I hate the thought of her wasting her life in that room. She is so beautiful and bright. To see her pale and frightened with that haunted look in her eyes…"

It was a sad thought, but right now he needed to talk about Juliana. ''No other friends?''

Her lips quirked. ''Does my dad's secretary count?''

Her father's secretary might have given her support now and then, but he never would have been a confidant. ''No. He doesn't count.''

''How about the ladies of the charities?''

''Do they smile and laugh with you?''

''Sometimes.''

''How about sharing secrets?''

She shook her head. ''No. We're not that close. It's unnerving enough seeing lies about yourself plastered on the front of the tabloids. Seeing my real secrets there would completely undo me.''

He grimaced. It sounded as if he would be sending her back to a sad, lonely existence. He didn't like the thought. But he didn't know how to prevent it, either. He could hope she found another man who truly loved her. One who would cherish her and love his daughter. But the mere thought made his heart pound and his fists clench.

And thinking about her with another man reminded him of another subject he wanted answers on. ''Tell me about the man who tried to make you his path to power.''

She heaved a long, put-upon sigh. ''I'm not going to tell you about that, Griffon.''

''Yes you are. Because you still have questions you want to ask, and you're smart enough to know that if I don't get a few answers, neither will you.''

"I've already given you as many answers as you've given me."

"Maybe. But you have more you want to ask. And I want payment up front."

She snorted in disbelief.

He just smiled. "It's not a perfect deal, but it's the only one you're going to get."

She gave another one of her irritated huffs. "It was a long time ago, and there's not that much to tell."

"Tell me, anyway."

"Fine. His name was Brandon and he was—*is* the owner of one of the biggest corporations in Bjorli. Most women think he's tall and handsome and dashing. And sadly at one time, I made the mistake of thinking so, too." She made a self-deprecating face.

Satisfaction slid through him. He didn't want her harboring so much as an ounce of good feeling for the bastard. "Where did you meet him?"

"At a ball at the palace. I was twenty-two and he was thirty-five."

He raised a brow. "A little old for you, don't you think?"

She looked as if she was going to object, but midbreath, her shoulders slumped and she nodded. "Yeah, he was. But I didn't see it at the time. I just thought he was sexy. He was so commanding and worldly wise."

He looked at her skeptically. "As the chancellor's daughter weren't you surrounded by commanding, worldly wise men?"

She chuckled softly. "Yeah, I was. But none of them were interested in me. I think most of them didn't even want to think about my father's wrath should they upset me."

He cocked his head in thought. "I thought you were afraid of men wanting you so they could be close to your father's power. Now you're saying men avoided you because of it?"

She smiled wryly. "It is a double-edged sword."

Now that she'd pointed it out, he imagined it was. "But your father didn't scare...slime-bucket, huh?"

She laughed wickedly. "I like that. And no, my father didn't scare ol' slime-bucket. He was quite sure of himself. Sure that he could keep me happy. And in the dark. Sure he could court my father's favor and use the crown's power to his advantage." She shook her head, as if marveling at her gullibility. "He was *so* smooth. He smiled when he was supposed to smile, flirted when he was supposed to flirt and stroked my bruised, uncertain ego at every opportunity. I thought he was so romantic."

Her laughter was cold and bitter. "Lord, was I an idiot."

Griff hated the idea of some man building Juliana's dreams when he had no intention of fulfilling them. And the idea of some man seducing her to get what he wanted made him want to kill the bastard. He tightened his hand around his glass until he was surprised it didn't break. But he made sure he kept his voice even. "How did you find out differently?"

She made a face and dropped the uneaten portion of her sandwich back on his plate, then brushed her hands off as if disposing of a nasty substance. "I stopped by his office one night. It was late, his secretary and everyone else was gone, but I knew he wouldn't be. He always worked late."

She paused, and her lips turned down as she gathered the unpleasant thoughts. "It was the anniversary of the evening we'd met. I wanted to celebrate. So I brought a few hors d'oeuvres and a bottle of champagne." She shook her head again. "I wanted to surprise him, so I tiptoed down the hall. But as I got close to his office I heard voices. I froze on the spot, wondering if I should just sneak back out or sally forth and demand whoever it was leave so we could have our celebration."

She shifted against the Jeep. "I don't know what kept me from doing either, but instead I sneaked closer, straining to hear what was going on in the office. As I got nearer I realized Brandon was talking to the vice president of his company. Then I realized what they were talking about."

She paused again, but this time she didn't go on. She sat silently against the truck, her face filled with the shock of the betrayal she'd discovered that night.

He nudged her gently. "What were they talking about?"

"Going global. With my father's connections. The connections they would acquire through me. They were already celebrating with their own bottle of liquor. I heard the neck of the bottle clink against their glasses as they poured the next round. Even today I can picture them lifting those glasses to make their toast." She lifted her own glass, imitating the gesture. "'To Juliana Bondevik, my future bride, and our golden goose.'" She went pale as she spoke the words. Even years later the slime-bucket's betrayal hurt her deeply.

Just as his own betrayal had.

Damn, damn, *damn.*

"I was such an idiot." Her whisper fell between them. "I realized then that love wasn't going to happen for me. That no man was ever going to want me just for myself. My connections are just too big a lure."

His gut twisted. "That's why you registered at the lodge as Smith, wasn't it? So you'd know whatever man you met would be after you and not your connections."

She managed a small smile. "Well, actually, I wasn't there man hunting. But yes, I had gone there to get away from the whole chancellor's daughter thing. It had been four years since slime-bucket had made his bid for greatness on my title, and it seemed that everyone, particularly every man I'd met in the ensuing four years, wanted to do the same thing. I was feeling down and cynical—as if I was losing myself. So I ditched my guards and my poor parents and ran away to the lodge to be Juliana Smith for a few weeks.

"I wanted—needed—to be accepted for *who* I was, not *what* I was. I figured if no one talked to me at the lodge, fine. But if a few people did choose to speak to me, at least I knew they were doing it because they liked *me.*"

He thought of the loneliness he'd seen in her eyes when she'd brought him that cup of hot cocoa. Now, he knew what had put it there. He closed his eyes against the picture. "And then I did a lot more than talk." Remorse colored his words.

She smiled sadly. "Yeah."

God, he was as bad as slime-bucket. Someone should string him up and feed him to the buzzards. He opened his eyes and turned his gaze on her. "You do know I didn't use you at the lodge, don't you?" The words were a hopeful plea.

"I think I know, but it doesn't really matter."

He didn't like the word *think*. And he liked the phrase *it doesn't really matter* even less. He didn't want her to *think*. He wanted her to *know* she'd been cherished. For *who* she was, not *what* she was. He didn't give a rat's ass about her sovereign connections. He wanted only to give her back those two weeks as a good memory and not a bad one. "It matters."

She laughed humorlessly. "How do you figure? There isn't a future for us. You want me to go home and pretend you're dead, for pity's sake. What possible difference could it make?"

Those two weeks were all he would ever have of an impossible dream. As such, they meant the world to him. On dark, lonely nights he trotted them out and relived them moment by moment. If Juliana was going to spend the rest of her life in a big, lonely palace, she deserved to have those two weeks to get her through the darkest nights. "It makes a difference to me."

Chapter Twelve

"Shhh, baby, it's okay." Juliana bounced the baby on her shoulder as she strode, for the thousandth time, across the oriental carpet covering the living room floor. The midmorning sun shone through the windows on the second day in the cabin. A day Juliana had planned to be joyous and fun. It was turning out to be anything but.

Perry was getting a new tooth.

Juliana stuck her finger in the baby's mouth so she'd have something to gnaw on. "Hang in there, sweetie pie, the painkiller I gave you should be kicking in any minute." She certainly hoped so. It had been a long night. She was tired and a headache pounded at her temples.

And poor Perry wasn't having any fun, either.

But she was blissfully quiet now as she chewed on

Juliana's finger. Unfortunately, she tired of the human offering just as quickly as she'd tired of everything else Juliana had offered her to chew during the night. Pushing the finger away, Perry switched back to her unhappy cries.

Juliana sighed and put a little more spring in her step. A little help here would be nice. Someone to take the baby for a while to give her a short break. But where was Griffon?

Out on the porch, pacing back and forth like a caged panther.

She sighed. He was still avoiding the cabin as if it was the pit of hell. Since she'd spent the night trying to soothe Perry she hadn't had time to figure out a way for Griffon to see the cabin differently. To see it as a home. And if Perry didn't give her a break so her brain could quit pounding and start thinking, she'd never figure it out. Besides, as long as Griffon was out there and they were in here, he was never going to get to know his daughter.

She glanced out the window just as Griffon strode by for the hundredth time.

This was ridiculous. This whole plan was falling apart at the seams. Maybe there wasn't anything she could do about his feelings for the cabin right now, but she could certainly do something about him running away from his daughter. The man had two good arms, and it looked as if he wasn't going to stop pacing any time soon. He might as well be carrying his daughter while he did it. It wasn't like handing him the baby would disturb his peace. He didn't seem to have any. And maybe, just maybe, if he spent a few minutes with his daughter in his arms, he might find some. At the very least, *she'd* get some much-needed rest.

She strode to the door and pulled it open.

Griffon swung toward her, his expression tight. "What's wrong with her? Why won't she quit crying?"

"Is that why you're out here? Because Perry's crying?"

He ran his hand down his face. "I told you I can't breathe in there."

Yes, he had. But she was in no mood to sympathize with his problems. "Well, you're out here now. You ought to be able to breathe just fine. And your baby's crying because she's getting a tooth."

A tad of impatience invaded his expression. "Is that all? Did you try giving her something to chew on?"

She rolled her eyes. "Gee no, it never occurred to me. But since it occurred to you, maybe you'd better take her." She stepped forward to give him the baby.

He backed up as if she was offering him a hot coal. "No."

"Yes. I have one crybaby on my hands, I'm not listening to another. She's yours." She put the baby right up next to his chest and let go.

As she knew he would, he caught Perry before she'd fallen half an inch. He hefted the baby as if he'd done it a hundred times, settling her in the crook of his arm as he shot Juliana a black scowl. "What's wrong with you? What if I'd dropped her?"

She rolled her eyes again. "You weren't going to drop her, Griffon."

His scowl didn't ease a bit. "You're awfully sure of yourself. And what was that little remark about crybabies supposed to mean?"

"It means I'm not listening to you try to avoid your daughter any longer. I was up half the night trying to keep her quiet so you could sleep. I'm tired and cranky and I have a headache. I need a nap. So it's your turn to watch her for a while."

His brows crashed together in alarm. "Weren't you listening yesterday when I said I was afraid of hurting her?" Desperation filled his words.

But she refused to be swayed. "Of course I heard you. But I don't believe it. And—"

"It's not up to you to decide if you belie—"

"*And* while I admit I don't know much about a soldier's life, I know those hands, Griffon." She pointed to the big, strong hands cradling Perry's small body. "They're gentle and unbelievably tender. They're not going to hurt her. And neither are you." She strode back into the cabin, closed the door behind her and dropped the big board into the lock position. She leaned against the rough panel. What a mess. But she was doing the right thing. She *was*.

If Griffon wasn't going to spend time with his daughter on his own, she was going to have to force his hand. She wished for him and Perry that this road was easier. More filled with laughter and smiles than tears and tension. But they'd had only four days. And they were down to three now. She had to use that time the best she could.

And she had to rest, clear her brain, so she could come up with a plan to bring Griffon inside, show him what a real home was, show him how important a part he could play in his daughter's life.

Griffon stood on the porch, staring at the closed door.

His heart pounded. A cold sweat covered his body. And Perry wailed in his ear as she, too, stared at the door her mother had just disappeared behind. He briefly thought about kicking the damned thing down and handing Perry back to Juliana with a few choice words about her cavalier attitude toward her daughter's safety. But he was afraid the action would scare Perry. And he didn't want to do that.

He shifted Perry in his arms. Now what?

He jostled the baby, trying to quiet the wail. "Come on, little one, shhh. Your mommy's tired and needs to sleep. And if you don't stop that caterwauling, it's never going to happen." And we *need* it to happen so she can wake up and feel better, and I can get you back into the safety of her arms.

But his plea fell on deaf ears. The only thing Perry seemed able to think about was her sore mouth. She shoved her fist in it and cried around her fingers while she gnawed furiously on them.

Panic and tension built in him like steam in a boiler. He was surrounded by every trigger that had sent his father into his fits of rage. Close quarters. A tense situation. A crying baby. And Juliana had just handed this tiny, fragile being into his care. The pressure pushed hard against his chest, but he tightened the hatches on it. Nothing was going to happen here. He'd dealt with crying babies before. He could do this without losing his cool. He *could.*

Drawing a desperate breath, he strode off the porch. "How about a walk in the woods? Maybe we'll find something that will get your mind off your sore mouth." And the movement would be good for him.

He made his way to the woods in big, buoyant steps, hoping to lull Perry. But while her crying slowed a bit, it certainly didn't stop. Spotting a crow sitting on a branch, he stopped and pointed to the bird. "Looky there, sweetheart. A crow."

Perry wasn't impressed, and when she realized they were no longer moving, she wailed louder. The crow flew away with an indignant flap of its wings.

He quickly moved back into his rolling walk. "Okay. Don't like crows, huh? How about chickadees. There's one over there. Look." He pointed to a small bird sitting on a nearby bush.

This time, the unhappy tyke actually looked. And her crying actually subsided. For a whole ten seconds.

"Okay. Don't like chickadees, either. How about..." He wove around a bush, looking for another specimen.

Ten minutes later Perry was still crying and he'd pointed out every bird and squirrel in the forest. To no avail. Man.

A bath had always been a good diversion to get his brothers and sisters to quit crying, but there wasn't even a tub in this stupid cabin. And Juliana was in there, anyway, trying to rest. He couldn't very well bring the crying Perry in there even if there had been a tub.

He looked around the woods, his gaze falling upon the stream. *Yeah.* "Would you look at that, sweetheart. A stream. Wouldn't you like to check out the stream? Sure you would. Because if this diversion doesn't work, we're sunk." But it was going to work. It *had* to work. He was afraid his nerves had taken just about all the crying they could.

He strode over to the stream and set Perry down on the ground next to it. "Look at that water. Isn't it pretty?"

Perry startled when he set her down, her wails stopping midcry. The gurgling water seemed to catch her attention, and she sup-supped as she watched it.

Quickly, before she lost interest, he sat down beside her and ran his fingers through the shallow brook. "Look how it sparkles."

Perry watched his fingers trail through the water.

"Cool, huh. Wanna try?"

She sat quietly watching, but didn't seem inclined to dabble her own fingers.

Hoping for a little better reaction—one that might actually cheer her up and make her forget about her teeth—he picked a small stone off the bottom and tossed it toward the middle. It landed with a soft plunk.

Perry smiled.

Yes. He picked up another pebble and tossed it. It landed a little closer, and since it was bigger made a bigger splash.

Perry laughed.

Yes, yes, *yes.* "Okay, your turn." He plucked another smooth stone from the brook and handed it to Perry.

She immediately raised it to her mouth.

"No, don't eat that. It's yucky." He made a face to indicate such. "Throw it."

She gurgled, looked at the stone and then back to him.

"Go ahead, throw it." He mimicked the action.

She gave it a mighty toss—for a twelve-month-old. It landed right in front of her with a pretty good splash. She startled as the water hit her.

He held his breath, praying she was a good sport. Praying the splash hadn't just ruined everything and she would start crying again.

She shivered once, her eyes wide with surprise, and then a smile broke out on her face and tiny giggles rippled into the air.

He let out the breath he'd been holding. "You liked that, huh? Here, let's get you another one." He handed her another stone.

Unfortunately she tired of that game quickly. And turning her nose up at the fifth stone he offered her, she started crawling for the stream instead, bigger adventures on her mind.

"Oh, no." He grabbed her. "You're not going in there. You get that pretty dress wet, your mom will skin me alive."

She squirmed against his hold and started to wail in protest.

He shuddered at the sound. "But then again, your mom put you in my care. And I don't care if you get the danged thing wet.'' He opened his hands. ''Go for it kid.'' Thankfully the water wasn't too cold. This little brook was so shallow the summer sun kept it tepid.

She crawled fearlessly into the shallow brook, nothing but happy sounds tumbling from her now. When she reached the middle of the stream she looked back at him, an expectant look on her face.

He laughed softly. ''No way I'm joining you in there. As you will discover in due time there's nothing worse than wet sand in your pants. I'm staying here.''

Since he didn't follow her, she obviously decided she'd crawled in far enough. Sitting down, she started having fun. She picked stones from the bottom of the stream, tossed them, and during quieter moments just held her hands in the water, watching the frolicking current play over them.

He sat on the edge of the bank and watched as she splashed and laughed and played. With every happy coo, every exuberant laugh, his tension eased and something warm and light and comforting took its place. He loved watching her slap at the water. There was just something about her uncoordinated movements backed by her unencumbered zeal that touched his heart. And the fat crystalline drops of water that clung to her chubby cheeks and short, black lashes made him think of marshmallow bunnies with sugar crystals sprinkled on them. Too cute.

She grabbed a stone from the bottom of the river and put it in the natural pocket her skirt made as it hung between her legs. Deciding she liked it there, she started adding to the cache with several other stones and a good portion of the river bottom.

He shook his head. If he didn't do something quick, she was going to be a sandy mess. He pushed up from the bank and waded into the water. "Hey, sweetheart. I think you've had enough of the stream." He picked her up, dumping the stones from her dress and giving it a quick swish in the water before he headed for the bank.

Taken away from her fun, Perry started squirming.

"Don't panic, we'll think of something else fun to do." He wasn't sure what yet, but he'd come up with something. He didn't want those smiles to disappear. He plopped her on the bank and quickly searched for another diversion. Little presented itself. But there were plenty of stones. He started stacking some of them beside her. "We can play with the stones here. Just don't put them in your dress. Okay?" He started stacking some of the pebbles strewn around the bank beside her. "We can build stone…castles." Yeah, castles sounded good. All little girls liked castles, didn't they?

At least Perry seemed to. She watched intently as his castle grew. And soon she started adding pebbles of her own. When the pile got to the point the stones were tumbling off, she crawled over and started another one. He went with her and helped with the next castle. She looked up at him, smiling and babbling something very interesting if the expression on her face meant anything.

His heart squeezed. She was so…happy and innocent and full of trust.

And she was his.

At least for this moment.

Juliana's words echoed in his head. *She'll know, Griffon. If you really spend time with her, playing with her, talking with her, instead of just staying with us in the cabin, she'll know. Deep in her heart, deep in her soul, she'll know that at one point in her life her father cared for her.*

He stretched out on his belly and propped himself up on his elbows, so they would be eye to eye. He picked up a stone and added it to the pile. "You know, your mom seems to think if we spend a little time together, you'll remember. Not the words, or even the moment, but that somewhere inside you, you'll remember...something...of the time we spent together. I'm not sure I believe her. I'm afraid your old man has a rather more...jaded outlook on life. But just in case she's right..." Tears stung his eyes. "Your daddy loves you. With all his heart. And all his soul. And all his being."

A lump lodged itself in his throat, making it hard to speak. But he cleared his throat and forced the words through the stricture. "I think you're beautiful and wonderful and bright. And I'll be watching—not from anywhere you can see me—but I'll be watching for anyone who says or thinks differently. I'll make sure they don't bother you. I'll make sure you'll always have everything you need. I promise."

Footsteps sounded behind him. He glanced in the direction of the cabin.

Juliana strode through the woods toward them, her

hair swaying softly with every step, a bit of color back in her cheeks.

He cleared his throat, making sure she wouldn't hear the emotion he'd just shown his daughter. He felt awkward enough telling his daughter he loved her. He didn't want anyone else in on the conversation. Even Juliana. Giving Perry a smile, he sat up and gave Juliana a nod. "You look better."

"I feel better, thanks. And thanks for watching Perry."

He snorted, remembering the high-handed way she'd handed the baby off. "Like I had any choice in the matter."

She gave him a totally unsympathetic smile. "You survived." She looked at Perry. "And she looks happy."

He looked at the baby playing, piling her pebbles high. She was happy.

And he'd been the one to create that happiness. His heart squeezed again, and a tiny bit of pride warmed him from the inside.

"What are you two building?" Juliana tipped her head toward the stone pile.

He smiled as Perry added another stone. "Stone castles."

"Castles, huh?" Humor sparkled in her eyes as she gave the shapeless piles a skeptical look. "You could maybe talk me into believing they're the archeological *ruins* of castles built long, long ago."

He shot her a mock affronted look. "You, my lady, have no imagination."

She chuckled softly. "Guess not." Rocking back

on her heel, her gaze skated over him. "Correct me if I'm wrong, but you look like you're having as much fun as Perry."

He was having fun. So much fun his heart ached with it. Ached because three days from now he'd have to put both Perry and her mother on a plane and wave goodbye. Forever.

But he didn't have to do that today. Thank God, not today.

Or tomorrow.

And between now and then he was going to spend every moment he could with this tiny miracle.

With Perry *and* Juliana. He wouldn't have to worry about hurting the child if he was with Juliana. She would never let him hurt their child.

He nodded his head. "I am having fun. *We're* having fun." He waved his hand between Perry and himself. "Sit down and join us."

Juliana had a plan to, hopefully, give Griffon an idea of what a home was. It wasn't a great idea. In fact, it was pretty pitiful. But she was running out of time. And stuck in the middle of a military installation, she didn't have a lot of tools at her disposal to improvise with. But she could come up with flour and shortening. And she'd noticed an apple tree laden with apples down by the stream.

She smiled as she thought of the scene she'd found this morning when she'd wandered down to find Perry and Griffon. She wasn't sure what had happened between daughter and father during that time, but Griffon's attitude had shifted. She wasn't exactly sure how. But it had changed. And definitely for the better.

She didn't get the impression, however, that he intended to change his mind about sending them home and never seeing them again. But he'd definitely decided to spend time with Perry here, now. He'd told Juliana he didn't want to be left alone with the child again. Which was fine with her. If it made him feel better to have her around maybe he'd relax more and share more of himself with his daughter. And Juliana enjoyed watching them together.

She sighed in frustration. For a man who seemed so afraid he'd hurt children, he seemed to have an uncanny way with them. He knew how to pick them up, feed them, even tease them out of their nasty moods. How could he possibly believe he was an unfit parent? From everything she'd seen, he'd make a bang-up dad.

She shook her head. She wasn't going to harp on that problem now. She had a different obstacle to tackle. Showing Griffon what a home was about.

She stepped out onto the porch.

He looked over from where he sat on the porch's old railing, staring out into the woods. "Is Perry asleep?"

She nodded. "She should be down for a good two hours. Maybe three. So I thought you and I should make a pie."

He looked at her as if she'd lost her mind. "What?"

"You heard me. We're going to make a pie."

His look got a little more skeptical. "'We'?"

"Yeah. You. And me."

He shook his head. "You're out of your mind."

The blunt assessment startled her, but then a slow smile curved her lips.

He gave her a suspicious look. "What is that smile for?"

"You know, no one would ever tell the chancellor's daughter she was losing her mind. Even if that person were joking." And she wasn't at all sure he was joking. Her smile got a little wider. "I like it."

Now he *really* looked at her like she was crazy. "Yeah, well, I'm glad you're happy. But I'm still not going to help you make that pie."

She gave him her most innocent smile. "Of course you are."

"Of course I'm not. I'm a soldier, Juliana. I don't make pies."

She kept her smile firmly in place. "Today you do."

"And why is that?" he asked cautiously.

"Because, it's not about making a pie. It's about doing something in this cabin. Something fun. So you can quit looking at the place like snakes are going to start crawling out of every crevice."

He pulled in a breath to protest.

She held her hand up, stopping the words before they'd crossed his lips. "Don't fight me on this, Griffon. You're going to lose."

"Don't bet on it."

She resisted the urge to shake him until his teeth rattled and ratcheted up her smile instead. "Listen, I want to make a pie. I have *always* wanted to make a pie. Unfortunately, since my mother doesn't cook and the chef in the palace kitchen shoos me out the second I walk through the door, I've never had the opportunity.'' She leveled her gaze on him. ''Today is that opportunity. A once-in-a-life-time opportunity. And I want to share it with you. You aren't going to turn me down, are you?'' She batted her lashes and delivered her coup de gras. ''The woman you supposedly cared about but left high and dry at a Swiss ski lodge, anyway?''

His eyes closed to narrow green bands. ''You play dirty, Juliana.''

She shrugged. ''Of course I do. I grew up cutting my teeth on palace intrigue and world politics. Now hand me the radio. I need to get someone up at the compound to bring us the pie ingredients.''

He stared at her—hard—as if he might refuse. But then he heaved a resigned sigh, swung down off the railing, his feet hitting the wooden porch with a hollow thunk, unclipped the radio from his belt and handed it to her.

She smiled in triumph and pressed the talk button. ''Hello, is anyone there?''

''Ms. Bondevik?'' A surprised voice crackled over the airwaves.

''Yep, it's me. Who's this?''

''Cash. Where's the major?'' A hint of worry tinted the man's words.

Griffon leaned back against the rail, crossing his arms over his chest. ''You better tell him I'm all right, or he's going to send a small army out to see if you've killed me and dumped my body somewhere.''

She'd pressed the talk button during Griffon's suggestion and held the speaker in his direction. Now she turned it back to her lips. "Did you hear that, Cash?"

"Yes, ma'am."

"Good. You can keep your small army up there then. But I want you to tell the cook to collect all the ingredients for apple pie and send a man to the cabin with them."

"Apple pie?"

She smiled at the disbelief in the man's voice. "Yep. Apple pie. Hurry, Cash. We only have nap time to get this done."

"Major?"

She shot Griffon a glance that clearly said he'd *better* tell Cash to get his obsequious little behind moving.

Griffon chuckled, unimpressed by her warning, but he tipped his head toward the radio. "Press the button."

She did and canted the radio toward him.

"Do it, Cash."

"You got it."

She shook her head and handed the radio back to him. "If you're done playing soldier, let's go pick the apples while we're waiting for the makings to arrive."

"Pick the apples? You just told Cash to bring all the ingredients."

"Well, call the guy back and tell him everything but the apples. You and I are going to pick those. Come on. You'll like this part. Plenty of air, no walls."

It didn't take them more than ten minutes to pick the apples and return to the cabin. She strode onto the porch and into the small house. She'd dumped her apples into a big bowl in the kitchen before she realized Griffon wasn't with her. She glanced over her shoulder for him.

He was standing in the open doorway, staring in, the strong lines of his face tight.

She turned to him, locking her gaze on his. "Come on, Griffon, don't quit on me now."

He drew a deep breath—and strode through the door. Joining her in the kitchen, he dumped his apples on the counter next to the bowl she'd filled and then turned to her, his expression grim, but game. "Okay. What's next?"

She gave him a reassuring smile. "Let's get these washed, peeled and sliced. Then, once the ingredients arrive, we'll be ready to go."

She tried desperately not to notice how good it felt to have his shoulder bumping against hers as they worked in the tight quarters. And she kept the conversation easy but constant as they washed the small, imperfect apples. She could feel the tension in his shoulders, see it in his face, and she wanted him to relax.

She grabbed another apple and dipped it in the bowl of water they were using to wash the fruit. "When I was a little girl my mother read us stories about the settlers who built these cabins. How they'd struggled together as a family to survive in the harsh realities of the frontier."

He tossed another apple in the clean pile. "You

sound almost wistful, like maybe you wouldn't have minded being one of them.''

"I don't think I would have. In fact, I often day-dreamed of it.''

He raised a brow. "I hate to tell you this. But I'm pretty sure fighting the Indians and trying to keep from starving to death in a hostile environment wasn't nearly as romantic as the stories made it out to be.''

"Oh, I'm sure it wasn't. But it wasn't the excite-ment of the Indian Wars or the drama of man against nature that caught my attention. It was the simple things the family did together that I envied. Doing chores together in the morning, feeding the horses and chickens, collecting the eggs, milking the cow. And there was often a scene where the mother and daugh-ter made pies or cookies together in a warm kitchen while the snow blew outside. I don't know, it just all sounded so…cozy and unencumbered.''

He gave her a dry look. "Homey?''

She chuckled softly. "Yeah. Homey.''

He shook his head.

But she noticed the hint of a smile pulling at his lips. He was teasing her. And starting to relax.

She didn't try to stop the smile that pulled at her own lips as she grabbed the last dirty apple from the bowl. "Once we have these cleaned we need to peel them and slice them up. By then the rest of the in-gredients should be here.''

She called it almost perfectly. They were just slic-ing up the last apple when they heard a Jeep drive up to the cabin. She nudged Griffon's shoulder. "Get the door before he knocks, will you? I don't want him to wake Perry.''

He laid his half-cut-up apple down and strode to the door.

She tensed a little when he disappeared onto the porch. He was probably just helping bring in the ingredients, but she didn't breathe easier until he returned to the cabin with Talon, both men's arms full of foodstuffs.

"Talon." She tipped her head in greeting.

The silent warrior tipped his own head back, but said nothing as he set his packages down and then disappeared back out the door.

She shook her head. "Could you like *order* him to talk to me? I'm not after his life story or deep, dark secrets, but a hello now and then would be nice."

Griffon chuckled. "Despite the military aspects of this installation and my position in it, in the end these men are mercenaries. They steer their own ships. So while I could certainly order him to speak to you, I wouldn't hold your breath waiting for him to actually do it."

She sighed. "Yeah, I was afraid of that." She dismissed the irritating warrior from her mind and turned her attention to the table. "Okay, pie time. The apples are sliced and ready to go. Now all we have to do is make a crust for them to go in." She stared at the ingredients before her. Flour, sugar, salt, cinnamon, shortening, butter. Hmm.

Griffon cocked his head, his brows pulled together in question. "Why are you just staring at that stuff?"

"I'm trying to figure out where to start."

"You don't have the first idea how to make a crust, do you?"

"Not really."

He gave a disbelieving huff.

She shot him a black scowl. "What? Just because I'm a woman I'm supposed to know how to make a pie? You think we're *born* knowing that stuff?"

"Didn't you just say mothers and daughters baked together on cold snowy days. You know the whole sharing, family thing."

"I said mothers and daughters *in those books* baked together. *My* mother hates cooking. *And* I always got chased out of the palace's kitchen. What about you?"

He gave her a blank look. "What about me?"

"Do you know how to make a pie?"

His eyes went wide—and then he laughed. Uproariously.

She startled at the unexpected sound. And then joy fluttered in her heart. At the lodge they had laughed together a lot. But she hadn't seen anything but dread and sadness in his expression since she'd arrived at his compound. And she certainly hadn't seen anything but tension in this cabin. He was definitely starting to relax now. Even have fun, if that laugh was any indication.

But the pie looked as if it was in serious trouble. "Well," she turned back to the table, "how hard can this be?" She studied the ingredients again. "We need a big bowl."

"On the way." He carried a bowl over from the counter, set it on the table and dropped into a chair. "Now what?"

What indeed? She picked up the nearest ingredient. "Flour. Let's start with flour." She poured a bunch into the bowl, the fine white powder mounding into a volcano-shaped pile.

Griffon watched her with growing worry. "You're not going to, like...measure that?"

"Why would I measure it, Griffon? I don't have a recipe. We're just going to put some of everything in the bowl and see how it looks."

"Mmmm, yummy."

She gave him a warning look. "It will be."

He smoothed the frown from his face. "Okay, it will be. What next?"

Lord knew, but she was just going to guess. "Salt."

"Salt it is." He picked up the salt box. "How much? A handful?"

"Oh, no. We're making a pie, not a science project."

Humor sparkled in his eyes. "You sure about that?"

"Oh, stop it." But she loved his teasing. Loved the hint of a smile on his lips, the sparkle in those green eyes.

A muffled cry echoed through the room.

They both froze, their ears straining, listening to see if there'd be another cry. Perry had only been down an hour, a short nap for her, but with her teeth, she could well be up.

Another cry, this one definitely serious, pushed its way through the heavy pine door.

Griffon pushed up from his chair. "I'll get her."

She stared at his retreating back. He was retrieving Perry? Without any prompting from her? Amazing. But good. Very good.

Smiling, she went back to the pie.

Griffon strode out of the bedroom, Perry perched on his arm, one of his fingers in her mouth. "Look, your mom's making a pie for dessert tonight. Do you like apple pie?"

Perry gurgled and chewed harder on his finger.

"This is going to be a very *special* pie," he expounded.

Juliana shot him another warning glance. "Be nice or you won't get any."

"I should be so lucky," he whispered to his daughter.

Smiling, Juliana added a big clump of shortening to the flour and salt.

Griffon grabbed the bowl of sliced apples from the kitchen counter and then joined Juliana at the table, Perry perched on his knee. "Here you go, sweetheart. Gnaw on this." He handed one of the apple slices to Perry as a substitute for his finger. A substitute Perry was more than happy with.

"Okay, two ingredients to go." Juliana added a handful of sugar and a few good shakes of cinnamon. Then she pushed the bowl in front of Griffon. "Here, you're the strongest. You stir."

He eyed the bowl doubtfully. "I'm not sure even I can whip that mess into submission."

Squelching her laughter, she managed to shoot him a quelling look.

But he wasn't fooled. With an easy chuckle he

started stirring. As he mixed the ingredients, the cinnamon turning the white mixture a dull brown, Perry reached over and grabbed a handful of the gooey stuff.

Griffon stopped stirring so he wouldn't catch her fingers. "You want to help, sweetheart?"

"Oh no." Juliana quickly pulled the bowl out of Perry's reach.

"Come on, Juliana, what can she hurt?"

"Griffon, if she helps, this pie is going to be a mess. And so will she."

He shrugged. "So what? She'll wash and...you don't really think this thing is going to be edible, do you?"

She booted his foot. "Yes, I do."

He looked at her with a sad expression. "Odd, I've never noticed this delusional side of you before."

This time she had to laugh. "Okay, I give up. You two have your fun." She pushed the bowl back in front of them and watched all hopes of the pie ever being edible fly out the window as two pairs of hands, one big and one small, mashed the gooey ingredients, squeezing it through their fingers and tossing it from one side of the bowl to the other until flour and shortening and specks of cinnamon were everywhere.

But she didn't care. This whole project had been about making Griffon comfortable in this cabin. About giving him a homey experience. And she'd done that.

His shoulders were relaxed. The lines of his face were relaxed. And he was smiling.

A smile that seemed to be contagious if her own

mouth stretching from ear to ear meant anything. But she couldn't help it. The sight of father and daughter sitting together, as if they'd done it all their lives, made her want to smile even bigger. And having all of them here, together, in the cabin, having *fun*... It was a scene right out of one of her pioneer stories.

Her heart hitched. This wasn't one of her pioneer stories. This was real life. Two days from now this moment would be only a memory. Tears stung her eyes, but she blinked them back. She wasn't going to think about that. Not now. She'd always dreamed of a moment like this. She wasn't going to waste it.

Chapter Thirteen

Juliana stood in the cabin's small bedroom, drawing in a deep, steadying breath. The smell of grilling steaks filling her nose. Griffon was fixing them a fancy meal. He'd said they needed something special to go with their pie. Not that they were going to eat that pie, but it was the principle of the thing, he'd said. And it had been an easy thing for him to do. The pie had had to go to the mansion for baking, so when Talon had returned with the finished pie, Griffon had him bring back a couple of steaks and a few dishes fixed by his cook to fill out the meal.

Juliana smiled. It had been a wonderful day. A perfect day. And she wanted it to end with a perfect evening. She smoothed the soft blue silk over her hip with a nervous hand. Griffon had said he liked pretty dresses. And this was one of her prettiest. Not her most seductive, because that's not where she wanted the night to go.

She'd ended up in Griffon's bed before she knew anything about the man once before, and it had gotten her nothing but heartache. She had no intention of repeating the folly. And while she knew a lot more about Griffon and his life now, he was still keeping secrets. Big, important secrets.

But she wanted to please him. Wanted to be pretty for him.

Silly. But she didn't think many people had gone out of their way to make Griffon Tyner's life pleasant or joyful. And she thought the time was long overdue. And part of her wanted him to look at her like a woman, not the mother of his daughter or the curse of his life.

Really silly. And a little dangerous. But she wasn't going to worry about that now. Today had been like a fantasy, the three of them here in this cabin like a real family. She wanted to hold on to that illusion for a little longer.

A light rap sounded on the door. "Juliana, the steaks are ready."

Her heart fluttered and she did a final check in the mirror. She loved this dress. Loved its double-layered construction, the way the sky-blue satin shimmered beneath the outer layer of sheer, icy-blue silk and the way the delicate color brought out the color of her eyes. And the style of the dress with its form-fitting top and flared, midcalf skirt made her feel soft and feminine and pretty.

Nervous anticipation skittered through her. She

hoped Griffon liked it. The V-neck was low enough to make a man notice, but not low enough to tease. And the small rhinestone buttons that danced down the front added an elegant touch of color and sparkle. She'd even put heels on for him. A pair of silver, strappy sandals that were much more pretty than practical. But that wouldn't matter. She didn't have far to walk, and pretty was definitely more important than practical tonight.

Another soft tap. ''Juliana?''

She spun away from the mirror, her nerves crackling. ''Coming.''

She stopped at Perry's crib, making sure the cherub was comfortably tucked in. Black lashes shadowed tiny cheeks, and her breathing was even and peaceful. The poor kid had had a tough day with the new tooth coming it. But the jagged edges of white enamel had finally broken through early this evening. After Juliana had fed her a good dinner the baby had crashed about an hour ago, exhausted from her hard day.

Okay, she couldn't procrastinate any longer. Drawing a deep breath, she left the bedroom.

Griffon was at the table putting their steaks on their plates.

She drew in another whiff of the grilled meat, her mouth watering. ''That smells wonderful.''

He turned from the table…and froze.

Everything except his eyes. Those widened in surprise, his dark-green gaze flying from the top of her head to the tip of her silver sandals before starting a slow, meticulous journey back up. By the time his gaze finally made it back to hers, it twinkled with pure male appreciation.

His lips twitched. "I thought your goal was to go home without ever having worn one of those dresses?"

She smiled and shrugged. "I won't tell if you won't."

"Absolutely not. Come on, sit down. Everything's ready." He crossed the room to her, his stride long and eager. Settling his hand in the small of her back, he escorted her to the table, his fingers stroking gently over the soft silk.

A tingle of awareness shimmered through her. She loved his touch. She always had.

At the lodge she had reveled in it. And he had been more than generous with his touch there, as if he couldn't get enough of her. When they were in public one of his hands had always been on her, at her elbow, the small of her back. And it never just rested there. It had moved restlessly, just as it did now, delivering a gentle massage, an intimate caress. And when they were alone...

She shivered, heat and desire sliding through her. Maybe she'd best not think about those times right now.

"Are you cold?" His hand rubbed over her back, as if he were trying to warm her.

She chuckled. "No. Definitely not." She moved away from his touch and quickly dropped into the safety of the nearest chair.

But the heat sliding through her didn't diminish a bit. And she feared it wasn't going to. The room's atmosphere was far too intimate. Griffon had obviously had Talon bring back more than a few food dishes. The table was set with fine china, fancy silverware, heavy crystal…and candles. Granted, the place had no electricity, and light had to be provided with either candles or a kerosene lamp. But still, the candlelight definitely lent a seductive quality she would have been better off without.

Griffon sat across from her, his motions stiff and a bit awkward as he spread his napkin in his lap.

Following his lead, she picked up her own napkin, her fingers clumsy as she unfolded the white linen. She tried desperately to ignore the sexual tension crackling between. But it was there. Like a live wire in a storm.

She cleared her throat. "You've set a beautiful table."

"I'm glad you like it." His gaze fell to her neckline, his eyes darkening.

A tingle of desire shot through her, warming her skin and making her nipples peak against the smooth satin.

His gaze darkened more, and his nostrils flared.

Oh, dear. This neckline was obviously more of a tease than she'd thought. For both of them. She took a deep, fortifying swallow of wine. "So, what kind of steak sauce do you like on your steak?" The question was deliberately ridiculous.

His gaze snapped up to hers, color climbing up his neck. He looked guilty and embarrassed, like a little boy who'd been caught stealing from the cookie jar.

She chuckled softly. "This is awkward, isn't it? I

think because it feels a little like a date. And we both know it isn't.''

He shook his head, a wry smile turning his lips. ''I should have thought how it would look before I had all the nice stuff brought down. But, I had such a wonderful day thanks to you, and I wanted to return the favor...do something that would make you happy.''

She smiled. ''I wore the dress for the same reason. To make you happy. You said you liked pretty dresses. I thought you'd like this one.''

''I do. Very, very much.'' His voice was rough, tight.

More heat slid through her, but she didn't try to hide from it this time. They'd both agreed this was a friendly dinner, nothing more. When the last sip of wine was gone they wouldn't have to worry about the other one wanting something more. ''I'm glad. Now, let's eat these steaks before they get cold.''

They laughed and dug into their meals, talking and enjoying the wonderful fare. The sexual tension slid in and out of the conversation, in and out of Juliana's consciousness, making every thing more defined. Making the food taste better, the candlelight look more beautiful, the individual moments seem longer and more precious.

She'd forgotten how good it felt to share company with a man she was attracted to. Forgotten how good it felt to have a man look at her with desire. It was wonderful. Even if it was just an illusion.

Long before she was ready for the evening to be

over, her tummy was full. She leaned back in her chair with a satisfied sigh. "That was so good."

He took a sip of wine. "I'm glad you liked it. I wanted you to enjoy it."

"Well, I definitely did."

She studied him across the table. The candlelight played across the chiseled lines of his face. So handsome. And cute. Not handsome cute, but endearing cute. He was fidgeting with his wineglass and his silverware and his plate, moving them here to there and back again. It was as if he had something to say but was uncertain how to begin.

She nudged his foot under the table. "What's up?"

He met her gaze, his expression apologetic and resolute. As if he knew what he was about to say was going to cause discourse, but he had to say it anyway. "Remember yesterday, when I told you it mattered to me how you felt about those two weeks in Switzerland?"

"Oh, Griffon, don't go there. I don't want to ruin the night with this. It's been a wonderful day. Perfect in fact. And I already told you I believe you about the lodge. At least I think I do."

"It's that word, *think*. I can't stand it. I want you to *know*. You gave me the best two weeks of my life. The last thing I want is for you to look back on that time and feel used."

She sighed in frustration, but she didn't say anything. She didn't want to fight about this tonight.

"Dammit." He leaned across the table, his gaze intense. "I want you to have something besides bad memories from that time."

"I have more than bad memories, Griffon. I have a beautiful baby girl. Remember?"

Shadows filled his eyes. "That's not what I mean."

She smiled sadly, the evening's pleasure slipping away. "I know. But you want me to change my feelings about a very hurtful event without telling me why. I don't know if I can do that."

His lips pressed into a hard, thin line. "Why I left isn't important."

"*Of course* it is."

Frustration flashed in his gaze. "Look at me. Can't you see the truth in my eyes. Can't you see how much I care for you? That I would *never* do anything to hurt you."

"I see pain there...and regret. But what I *hear*, Griffon, is you telling me to go back to Bjorli and pretend you're dead. What makes you think that won't hurt me? Or Perry?"

"You don't understand." Desperation sounded in his voice. "I'll only hurt you if you *stay,* if you keep me in your lives."

She shook her head. "Is this more of that I'm-a-soldier nonsense? Because if it is, I got to tell you—"

He thrust himself from the table, one hand slashing the air. "It has nothing to do with my being a soldier. It has to do with the way I was raised. With the blood running through my veins."

She went still, her gaze boring into him. Had she finally pushed through his smoke screen? Was she finally getting close to his demons? "What does that mean? The blood running through your veins?"

Even in the candlelight she could see his skin pale.

He obviously hadn't meant to say that. Frustration must have pushed the admission from his lips. Spinning on his heel he strode from the table into the shadows of the room.

She jumped up from her seat and raced after him. "Oh no, you are not backing out of this now." She grabbed his arm, turning him back to her. "I want an answer. *Now*. What does the way you were raised and blood running through your veins have to do with anything?"

His face was a mask of anger and frustration and pain as he faced her. "What do you want to hear, Juliana? That I was raised by a man who used his family as a punching bag? A man who got his greatest pleasure by using his fists on his family. By making his family grovel in fear, cry out in pain? That as a child I hid myself and my brother and sisters in the closets praying to God he wouldn't find us?"

She dropped his arm and took a step back, her stomach turning, her blood crashing to her toes. How had he survived such a brutal childhood? Her stomach churned and her heart ached. She drew a shaky breath and licked her suddenly dry lips.

He laughed coldly. "Don't go anywhere yet. I'm just getting to the good part. You want to hear how, at fifteen, after a lifetime of hating that mean bastard, a lifetime of swearing I'd *never* be like him when I grew up, my brother pissed me off one day and I took my anger out on him just like my old man would have? With my fists. Is that what you want to hear?"

She took another step back, pain for that lost little boy slashing through her.

He shook his head, disgust directed purely at himself curling his lips. "Don't worry, Juliana. I'm not going to hurt you." His words were as cold and forlorn as the winter wind whispering over the North Sea.

Hurt her? What… "Wait a minute. *That's* what this is about? *That's* why you left me at the lodge? Why you want me to tell your daughter you're dead? Because you're afraid you're going to *hit* me? Or Perry?"

He looked down at her arm, the one that had been touching him and dropped away when he'd told her his story. "And you aren't?" He strode away from her.

"No." He would *never* hurt her. She knew it clear down to her bones. She ran after him again, turning him back to her. "You surprised me." Tears stung her eyes, but the pain slicing through her chest was nothing compared to the pain she saw in his face. The pain and shame. Shame for the ugliness of his past. Shame for giving in to his own weakness and frustration on the day he'd hit his brother.

Her heart ached for him. She wanted to tell him that he was being ridiculous. That she knew he'd never hurt anyone. That she'd only felt badly for the little boy. For the man. But one look at his expression told her he wouldn't hear her. And his pride wouldn't appreciate her sentiments if he did. But she had to make that look on his face go away. She had to.

And she knew only one way to do it.

Her heart raced. This wasn't smart. Not smart at all. But Griffon needed it. And…

She wanted it.

She wanted those memories from Switzerland and whatever ones they created tonight for the lonely days ahead. "Forget it. Forget all that. Show me..." She laid her hand on his arm. "*Show* me—don't tell me—how much you cared for me at the lodge."

He went still, his eyes darkening, his nostrils flaring. But he didn't move.

She stroked his shoulder. "Please, Griffon. Give me back those memories. Every word. Every touch. Every moment."

Griffon stood, paralyzed. Shock streaking through him. Heat and need following close behind. But she couldn't possibly mean... Not after what he'd just told her.

She moved closer, her pretty little silver shoes nudging his boots. Her heat soaking into his skin. Her breasts brushing against his chest.

Oh, she did. "Didn't you hear anything I just said?" He tried to pull away from her.

But her grip tightened on his arm and her steps matched his as he took a step back. "Yes, but I don't want to talk about it. I don't want to argue about it. Not now. Please." She raised on her tiptoes and sipped at his lips. Little butterfly kisses of enticement and entreaty. "Please."

Every muscle in his body snapped tight. In protest. In need. After what he'd just told her, she should be running the other way. But she wasn't. For whatever reason. She wasn't.

And with her lips on his, her body pressed against

his, he couldn't, either. Even with every sane molecule of his brain protesting, his body leaned down, his lips nibbling back at hers. "This is a mistake."

"I don't care. Do you?"

"No. Heaven help me, no." She was giving him the chance to show her how much those two weeks had meant to him. Giving him the chance to taste her sweetness one last time. Giving him the chance to save those memories for her. Tomorrow would be soon enough for everything else. He closed his lips over hers.

He'd thought of her, wished for her, dreamed of her for two long years. And now she was here, in his arms. Fire, white-hot and lightning quick, licked at his desire. He wanted her under him. Naked. Now. He started backing toward the bedroom, pulling her with him, his lips never leaving hers as he tasted her again. Her generousness, her sweetness, her passion.

But halfway to the bedroom he stopped with a frustrated groan. Breaking the kiss, he rested his forehead against hers, his breathing fast and hard. "We can't go into the bedroom. Perry's in there."

She ran her tongue over his bottom lip, her breathing as short and labored as his. "No problem. Here's good. The floor works."

He shook his head, frustration pouring through him. "No, it doesn't. We spend the night down there, you'll have rug burns. You'll feel ravished, not cherished."

She laughed, low and sexy. "The rug is silk, Griffon. There won't be any burns. And I'm going to be very disappointed if I *don't* feel ravished."

Heat surged through him. End of discussion. He dragged her over by the sofa, his heart pounding almost as hard as his need. He took a deep breath, trying to slow the blood rushing through his veins. If he didn't slow things down, this was going to be a damned short event. And he didn't want that. Shoving the coffee table next to the sofa, he made a wide space for them between the table and hearth. He glanced at the cold, empty fireplace and shook his head. "I would have laid a fire if I'd known, it would—"

She put her finger over his lips. "Shhh. Stop worrying. This isn't about the perfect time or the perfect place. It's just about you and me."

"Yes." He took her face between his hands and nibbled at her lips, small, teasing little kisses.

With a frustrated moan she nipped at his. "More."

He chuckled. "Soon." Sinking to his knees, he pulled her down with him. "I want to see you."

She blushed a very becoming shade of pink, but her hands went to the top button of her dress. Slowly, a little bit self-consciously, she began to unbutton one sparkly button after the other.

He wanted to tell her to hurry. He wanted to help. But he did neither. Anticipation was half the fun. And he didn't want to hurry her. She could take her time. They had all night. So he sat back on his heels, watching, admiring every inch of smooth, satiny skin that slowly came into view, anticipating the final unveiling. His blood ran hot and heavy. The boldest part of him throbbed.

She stopped when she'd undone the button at her waist. But instead of slipping the dress from her shoulders, she hesitated, her fingers closing tight on the filmy blue material, an expression he couldn't quite name crossing her face.

Modesty? It caught him off guard. She hadn't been so shy at the lodge. But this was a different time. A different place. And he had no problem reassuring her. Encouraging her. He shot her a teasing smile. "Come on. You're killing me." His words were rough with desire, brimming with need, but they did their job.

Her lips twitched, a shy smile alighting there. And then she slid the dress from her shoulders and let it fall to her waist, where it caught and draped on the curve of her hip.

He sucked in a breath. Candlelight played over the delicate curve of rib to waist, alabaster skin and a pretty, light-blue bra of satin and lace. Her pink nipples showed through the lace, enticing him, teasing him, reminding him just how lush those breasts were. "Beautiful." He waited with bated breath and rushing hormones for her to remove the scrap of lace, to show herself to him in all her naked glory.

But she made no move to remove the icy-blue confection.

Sweat beaded on his upper lip. He couldn't wait a moment longer. He had to see her. With shaking hands he undid the front clasp of her bra, pulled it open and slid the straps down her arm. "So beautiful."

The pink tinge in her cheeks darkened, and she looked away. "Not as beautiful as before. Having a baby takes its toll."

That's what the hesitation had been about. She was worried that having their daughter had changed her, made her less desirable? He shook his head. "It only made them more beautiful. Far more beautiful." He ran a finger along the outside of one soft globe.

Goose bumps ran over her skin, and her nipples peaked.

He smiled. "Still sensitive, I see." He cupped the heavy mounds in his hands, feeling their weight, reveling in their erotic pliancy. She felt so good. So damned good. He rubbed his thumbs over the rosy peaks.

She gasped in pleasure, her nipples turning harder against his thumbs. "Griffon?" She leaned into him, the whispered plea breaking on her lips.

He closed his mouth over hers and carefully lowered her to the floor. "Let's get this pretty dress off." His fingers made quick work of the next few buttons, and then he was pulling the silky material over her hips.

She gave him a strategic wiggle to help with the task and then started to jerk his T-shirt from his pants. "Come on, fair is fair. Get this thing off."

He quickly stripped his T-shirt off over his head, tossed it aside and reached for her blue panties.

She reached for his belt buckle.

He closed his hand over hers. "Nope. Leave those on for a while."

She groaned in disappointment. "Come on. If I'm going to be naked, I want you naked, too."

"Sorry. I'm too close to the edge. I need the deterrent."

"Oh, no—"

He shook his head. "Don't argue."

She shot him a wicked, sexy grin. "What if I do?"

He chuckled, slipping the blue satin off her feet. "You'll miss all the wonderful things I have to say about you. So be patient. Your job right now is to lie back and listen, very carefully, to what I have to say."

Absolutely, gloriously naked, she lay beside him, her hair spread out around her, her wicked smile making her eyes sparkle. "Hurry up. I'm waiting."

His whole body shook with need. He wanted to take her right now. Drive into her and show her with sheer force and enthusiasm how much she had meant to him. How much he wanted her—right at this moment. But he wasn't going to do that. He was going to go slow. Easy. Show her in exquisite, intimate detail just how beautiful, how amazingly special he thought she was.

Even if it killed him.

He sat beside her and touched a finger to the corner of her mouth. "I love your smile, more than almost anything else in this world." He dropped a soft kiss on her lips, wanting more. A lot more, but settling for the brief taste.

Her eyes sparkled with mischief and desire. "Almost?" she teased.

He smiled, bent down and drew one nipple into his greedy mouth.

She gasped, her back arching, her fingers digging into the carpet.

"I love that sound more. The sound of you gasping in pleasure." He suckled again, savoring the taste of her, the feel of her in his mouth. Blood raced to his arousal, making him pulse with need. But he ignored the almost painful ache. This was about giving Juliana her memories back. Not about how much he needed her. He drew her nipple into his mouth a little harder, rasping the hard nipple with his teeth.

A soft moan fell from her lips, and she reached for his knee, her fingers digging into his flesh.

"I love that sound even more. The sound of you moaning in pleasure. But what I love most of all is the sound of you crying out as you fly over the top." He dropped a kiss on the top of her breast. "But we're not going to get there for a while. A long while."

She groaned in frustration. "Stop teasing."

"But I love teasing you. And I love this spot." He touched a spot between her breast. "At the lodge you wore a cheap necklace you'd bought in one of the kid's gumball machines. A red string with a tin poodle hanging from it. And it used to nestle right here. I was so envious of that bloody piece of metal."

She gasped in surprise.

He raised a brow. "What? Did you think I had forgotten?" He ran his tongue over the spot, drinking in her heat, the light salty taste of her skin. "Never."

"It was just a dumb necklace. I'd almost forgotten it. I *had* forgotten it, until now."

"Well I didn't." He locked his gaze on hers. "I remember *everything*. Every day, every hour, every *second* of those two weeks."

She rolled her eyes. "At least the ones that had to do with your favorite body parts."

He shook his head. "*Every* one. I remember you were the most beautiful woman on the slopes." He dropped a kiss at the base of her neck and ran his hands down her ribs and over the soft curve of her hip, rediscovering her curves. Rediscovering her beauty. "The most beautiful woman in the world."

She sighed and stretched like a cat.

"I remember that you're not much for TV, but you're a sucker for an afternoon at the movies." He ran his hands back up her body, stopping at her breasts to run his fingers lazily around one of the delectable mounds, starting at the generous base and slowly...slowly inching toward her nipple. "And that nothing makes you hotter than the anticipation of a touch." The fact the anticipation was killing him he tried to ignore.

She whimpered and arched upward, inviting him, encouraging him to hurry and get to the good part.

"I remember you liked cream in your coffee in the morning and Amaretto in it at night. And that too much anticipation makes you growly and impatient." He tweaked the nipple that had been pouting for attention from the moment he'd touched her breast.

She arched hard again, drawing in a needy hiss.

He stretched out beside her, reveling in the feel of her skin against his, reveling in the sweet smell of her perfume, the musky smell of her arousal. He laved her nipple with his tongue and ran a greedy hand down her body.

Heaven on earth.

He drew a shaky breath. "I remember that you had a clear pink toothbrush with silver flecks in it. Like a little kid's. And that you like a soft, teasing touch...here.'' He dipped his fingers between her legs, his touch featherlight as it skimmed over the hard nubbin of her desire.

She closed her eyes on a moan and opened her legs for him.

He almost lost it when he felt her heat, her slickness. She was hot and wet and ready for him. But when she opened her eyes, it wasn't her passion that thrilled his senses. It was the realization in her eyes that if he'd remembered those details, he might—just might—have cared for her after all.

''So...damned...beautiful.'' He stroked her again as he closed his mouth over her breast.

She grabbed hold of his shoulders, pulling him closer as she pushed her hips up, seeking more of his touch, more of him. *''Griffon?''*

It was a pretty plea. A desperate plea. A damned sexy plea.

And he had long since gone beyond the moment when he could ignore it.

His hands were shaking so hard, getting his pants off was a challenge. But he managed. And then he was between her legs with nothing between them but sweat and heat and need.

She hugged her knees around his middle and wiggled. ''Hurry.''

He chuckled, a rough, rueful sound, but he didn't slide home. Gritting his teeth, he pulled back just enough to keep her seeking hips from their goal. ''Look at me.''

She groaned, opening her eyes and pinning him with a frustrated stare. "Quit playing. I *need* you."

She didn't have to tell him about need. But... "I just want to make sure we're clear on this. You understand I wasn't playing a game in the Alps. You understand I meant every word, every damned touch."

A slow smile turned her lips and a soft sheen of tears filled her eyes. "I understand."

"And you believe it."

"I believe it."

Griff couldn't have held out one more second. He pushed forward, sliding home until he was fully sheathed. Her heat surrounding him, his body intimately joined to hers, he held absolutely still, breathing in her scent, locking this moment away for all of time.

She wiggled against him. "Deeper."

Absolutely. He pushed in farther, claiming her.

She groaned, her fingers digging into his shoulders, pulling him closer still.

Sweat beaded on his brow, and need clawed at him like a ravenous beast, but using every ounce of willpower he possessed he resisted the urge to jump into a hard, quick rhythm. "One more thing." The three words were tight with need.

She groaned and nipped at his lips. "What now?"

"You understand as I lie here, buried deep inside you, that I don't give a good damn about your standing in Bjorli. That I'm not interested in your daddy or your position or your bloody power. That I'm interested only in *you*, Jules."

A single tear spilled over, running down her temple and into her hair. Her lips curved into a shaky, joyful smile. "You realize if you don't start moving—*now*—I'm going to kill you."

If he didn't start moving now, she wasn't going to have to kill him; he was going to die. He lowered his lips, tasting her, giving in to the fire racing through his blood.

She arched toward him, whimpering and pulling him deeper with every thrust. "Faster."

Oh, yeah. He increased the rhythm, doing everything in his power to keep his own skyrocketing desire from taking over as he pushed her closer and closer to the edge of release. His heart pounded, and his muscles shook and his ears strained, waiting, listening…

Her muscles grew tighter and tighter and then she snapped tight, flying over the top. *"Gri-i-i-ffon."*

The sweetest sound on earth.

He flew after her with a final, driving thrust.

Breathing hard, he gathered her close. His heart pounded.

Soared.

Ached.

He drew in a deep breath, inhaling her scent, inhaling the moment. She felt so perfect in his arms, her heat soaking into him, her heart beating with his. He tightened his arms, hugging her close.

Life wasn't going to get more perfect than this.

Juliana lay beneath Griffon, drinking in the feel of his heart pounding against hers, the sound of his labored breathing in her ear, the smell of his musk filling her senses. She wanted to steep herself in him. His smell. His heat. His strength.

She ran her hands down his back, relishing the hard muscle, the radiating heat.

He shivered and thrust into her once more. A slow, almost involuntary thrust of pleasure.

She shuddered with her own tingling aftershock and held him tighter. For the first time in her life she felt whole. She felt as if someone cared for *her*. Her head spun, her nerves sang and her heart trilled and ached at the same time.

This interlude wouldn't last. The day after tomorrow he'd put her on that plane and send her home. Which didn't mean she intended to stay out of his life. She definitely hadn't made that decision yet. But she wasn't going to argue that point now. For now she intended only to savor the moment. Every moment.

And she wanted Griffon to feel as wonderful as she did.

She couldn't imagine what it had been like to be raised the way Griffon had. To be raised by a man like his father. An angry beast who took his misery out on everyone around him. Her parents had never touched her in anything but love. Her parents had never even spanked her. A stern word and grounding had been her punishments. But Griffon...

And his mother had died when he was eight. He'd had no one to protect him from his father's wrath. Or comfort him after the punishing blows. Dear, dear Lord.

How did anyone survive being raised without the comfort of the human touch?

For the first time she understood why he liked to touch so much. He was soaking up the human contact. Contact he'd never had as a child. Or—as she was beginning to guess—never allowed himself as an adult. Her heart ached and she snuggled nearer.

Even now he had her gathered close, his arms caging her in both protection and reverence. As if she was a precious prize he didn't want to slip away.

She smiled and kissed his shoulder and the pulse throbbing at the base of his neck. And then she pushed at his chest. "Now it's my turn to make love to you." And when she was done there wouldn't be a spot on his body that hadn't been touched and kissed and oh, so thoroughly loved.

He raised a teasing, cocky brow. "What makes you think I'm up for it."

She chuckled softly, noting the telltale tensing of his muscles, the flexing of his manhood. "Oh, you're up for it."

Chapter Fourteen

Griff lay on the floor with Juliana in his arms, the morning light filtering through the cabin's small window, his heart aching and dread pressing down on him like a lead weight. She felt so right tucked into the curve of his arm. So right nestled against his body. But it was so wrong. So, so wrong.

What had he been thinking last night to take her in his arms? To make love to her? To let her make love to him? He'd wanted to erase all doubt about what had happened in Switzerland, yes. But this had not been the way.

And he'd been a fool to think it was.

All last night had done was make it harder for him to do what he must. Send Juliana and Perry back to Bjorli and never see them again.

Frustration and pain and anger pounded through his head. It was the last thing he wanted to do.

It was the only thing he could do.

But one more day of this familial bliss and another night of hedonistic abandon, and he'd never be able to do it. No way. No how.

He stared at Juliana's sleeping face, memorizing the way her lashes shadowed her cheeks, the way her lips curved in a soft smile, even in her sleep. He memorized the feel of her body snuggled against his, the way her knee curved possessively over his thigh, the soft press of her breast against his ribs. He memorized everything about this moment. And then he gently disengaged their bodies, pulled on his pants and started packing.

He smiled coldly as he tossed a pair of dirty fatigues into his duffle. He'd put himself between his father and his younger sister a hundred times, knowing it would earn him a beating. He'd marched into battles he'd never thought to walk out of. But this, making himself leave this woman and the tiny child sleeping in the next room, was the hardest thing he'd ever done.

But it was also the most important.

The most necessary.

Juliana woke when her head landed softly on the rug and the warmth left her side. Fighting through the lethargy invading her every muscle from the long night of lovemaking, she cracked her eyelids just enough to peer around the room.

Griffon stood by the sofa, shoving some of his belongings into his duffle.

A chill ran down her spine. Pulling the afghan they'd snuggled under last night over her breasts, she pushed herself up on an elbow. "Where are you going?"

"Back to the mansion." He didn't even turn around to talk to her. He just kept shoving things in his bag.

Panic grabbed her by the throat. "When will you be back?"

"I won't. I'll send Talon down to watch you two."

Her stomach clenched. This was Switzerland all over again. "Wait a minute." She couldn't let him just walk out of their lives. Not again.

Not after yesterday.

Not after last night.

She stood, gathering the afghan around her, tucking the edges in so it would stay. "Don't you think we should talk about this?"

"There's nothing to talk about."

Oh, yes there was. "Griffon, you can't keep making decisions for all of us on your own. It isn't fair."

He laughed humorlessly, his expression as dark as a thunderhead. "It's a lot more fair than the alternative."

She pulled in a deep, fortifying breath, preparing to face his demons head-on. "And the alternative is?"

"Me beating you. Or Perry. Take your pick."

"Oh, for pity's sake. You're being ridiculous."

His lips turned down, and she could see him preparing his next volley, but a cry from the next room interrupted.

They both froze, waiting to see if the cries would continue or if Perry would go back to sleep.

Another cry wafted from the room and was quickly followed by another. Perry was definitely up. And she wanted out of her crib.

Juliana tipped her chin toward the room. "You go get her. You wore me out last night. I don't think I can walk that far."

He snorted at her attempt to detain him. "You get her. I'm leaving."

Okay, she was going to have to do this the hard way. She counted to three...and jerked the duffle away from him. Racing to the other side of the coffee table, she gathered it next to her chest and closed her arms tightly over it.

He turned to her with a dark look. "Very adult."

She raised a disparaging brow. "And running away is?"

"In this instance, yes."

"Oh, please." She narrowed her eyes on him. "Go get your daughter, Griffon."

"I can leave the bag, Juliana."

"Of course you can, but then you'll have to fight your way over me to get out. And you wouldn't want to do that with Perry around, would you?" She was playing dirty again. But...

He stared at her long and hard, Perry's cries echoing in the cabin. And getting louder by the second. Finally he spun on his heel and disappeared into the bedroom.

She collapsed onto the sofa with a relieved sigh. She'd managed to keep him a few more minutes. But if she didn't think fast it would be a short victory. Lord, how on earth was she going to convince him he'd positively lost his mind if he thought he posed any danger to either her or Perry?

Thinking frantically, she listened to him talking to Perry as he changed her diaper and slipped her into a clean dress. His voice was easy, downright sunny as he spoke to her. If Juliana hadn't seen the dark look in his eyes moments before, the determination on his face, she'd never guess he was about to walk out on them again.

Griffon came out of the bedroom with a clean, smiling baby. Setting her carefully on the floor, he turned to Juliana. "You should feed her. I'm sure she's starving."

Juliana glanced at Perry. She was heading to the fireplace, her little green eyes sparkling with excitement. "I think she's more interested in hearing her voice echo through the chimney than she is in eating right now. Which is just as well. It will give us more time to talk."

"I'm not talking. I'm leaving."

She reasserted her grip on the duffle. "No you're not." She racked her brain, looking for a lead question. It took less effort than she thought. He'd singled out one moment in his past that changed his life. "I want you to tell me what happened with your brother when you were a teen."

He went pale, and his eyes turned almost black, as if they'd dropped into a bottomless pit. "No."

Her stomach turned. She was obviously asking him to dredge up bad memories. Horrible memories if his expression meant anything. But he wasn't giving her any choice. "You're going to have to, Griffon. Because I guarantee I'm not going to just waltz out of your life if you don't tell me."

"You won't have to waltz out. I'll send you. And prevent you from returning."

She laughed, shortly, humorlessly. "You're secure here from people parachuting in, are you?"

His eyes popped wide and then snapped to narrow, speculative bands.

She shrugged. "You know I'd do it. And even if I didn't, what's to prevent me from telling Perry you're here. Hale and hearty. Hiding from her. Then when she's old enough, *she* can parachute in."

Anger flashed across his face, and he stalked over to the sofa until he was looming over her. "You'd do that to your daughter? Tell her that her father was alive and well...and didn't want to see her? You'd do that, knowing how much it would hurt her?"

"If you don't start talking right now and convince me there's a reason you shouldn't be in her life, you bet your sweet little camo-clad derriere I would. I don't like the idea of lying to my child. If you want me to tell her you're dead, there'd better be a damned good reason."

She could see the fear in his eyes. Fear that she'd do exactly as she said, tell their daughter he was here, hiding in his compound. And give her the plane and the parachute, to boot. But he didn't start talking.

Apparently, it was going to take a little more pressure to get those lips moving. "I could always call my dad, have him talk to the king, have the king demand your president make you tell me."

He snorted at the outrageousness. "He's the president of the United States, Juliana, not my father or my boss. And he certainly has more important things to do."

"More important things than making sure his country stays at the top of the buyers list for Bjorlian oil? I doubt it. And he may not be your father or your boss but I think you have enough military background that if your commander in chief asks you to talk to me, you will. And trust me, with my connections, I can get him to ask."

He narrowed his eyes on her. "For all your complaints about being the chancellor's daughter, you obviously don't mind using that power when you need it."

"I pay dearly for the privilege, so you can forget about trying to make me feel guilty. Now tell me what happened with your brother."

"Nothing." Before she realized he'd even moved, he snatched the duffle from her arms and moved to the other end of the sofa with it. Setting it down, he started, once again, to shove his things into it.

She stared at him wide-eyed. Boy was he fast. She'd just lost her trump card. But she had other cards up her sleeve. Pure stubbornness for one. "Well, then we don't have a problem do we? What kind of visitation would you like to set up for Perry?"

He shot her one of his black little scowls.

"You can scowl at me until hell freezes over or

burns to the ground, soldier, but it won't change anything. We're going to have this conversation." Because it's important. My little girl's future happiness
depends on it. And so does yours, dang it. Can't you
see that? "So stop stalling and start talking."

He was trapped. And he knew it. The muscle along
his jaw ticked rhythmically as he grabbed his last be-
longing, crammed it in his duffle and zipped the bag
shut with suppressed fury. Straightening to his full
height, he stared down at her. "Dredging up ugly
stories isn't going to change anything. Or help anyone, either."

She prayed he was wrong. She had a daughter who
could definitely use the love of a father. And Griffon
desperately needed the love of a family. Even a long-
distance one if she couldn't talk him into anything
more. But she hoped to talk him into more. Much,
much more. For Perry's sake, Griffon's sake, and for
her own. "Why don't you start by telling me how old
your brother was when this event happened. I already
know *you* were fifteen."

"You're not giving up on this, are you?" Anger
and frustration sounded in his voice.

She shook her head.

He looked away, his expression hard. "Sean was
twelve. He had to stay after school on detention that
week, for pushing a girl on the playground. But he
was supposed to be home by five." His eyes took on
a faraway look, a haunted look as he dredged up the
old memory. "Dad was gone that night. He was gone
a lot, actually, thankfully. Anyway, I'd made dinner

and we were all waiting for Sean to come home so we could eat as a family.''

He shook his head and laughed, a single, humorless burst of sound. ''Some family. Four ragtag kids, scavenging for clothes and begging for food and pretending their lives were just like everyone else's. But when I was little, when my mom was well, she used to make dinner for everyone and we'd eat it together at the dinner table. Some nights Dad came to the table drunk and there would be hell and violence before dinner was out, but the nights he was gone it was nice. Just mom and us kids. It was one of the few peaceful times in our house. So I tried to keep that tradition alive after she'd passed on.''

Juliana's heart pounded and tears stung her eyes at the thought of a fifteen-year-old boy dodging his father's fists and working so hard to give his brother and sisters the one bit of happiness he'd had in his own short youth. She swiped at the tears, doing her best to keep her composure.

His already-dark look turned positively black, and he jabbed an angry finger at her. ''One more tear, and I walk out the door. I don't want your pity.''

She was sure he didn't. She was sure it pricked at his pride. But someone needed to cry for that little boy and the other children in that house. Unapologetically, she swiped at another tear. ''So walk out the door. I'll have the president on the phone within half an hour. And then we can start this all over again.''

''You've obviously forgotten how the phones work in my compound.''

"No, I haven't. But Talon will put the call through for me. You know how he loves everyone else's misery."

His grimace told her he did know.

"Go on, Griffon. You were waiting dinner for Sean, and…"

He paced away from the sofa, tension making his stride short and jerky. "Sean was late. I wasn't worried much when he wasn't home by five. But when six o'clock rolled around I sure as hell was. I took the girls and we went to the school, looking for him. But the lights were out and the doors locked when we got there."

His pace became quicker, more agitated as he remembered the fear he'd felt that night. "I became frantic and dragged poor Annie and Melissa all over the neighborhood looking for him, looking for anyone who might have seen him. But we came up empty. By the time we got back to the trailer at ten I was convinced some pervert had kidnapped him and tortured him to death. I was just dialing the cops for help when he came strolling into the trailer.

"At first I was so relieved to see him I nearly collapsed right there with the phone in my hand. But then the anger kicked in. We'd walked our feet off trying to find him. And now he was standing in the door, smiling, like nothing had happened. I slammed the phone back in its cradle and started yelling at him. Giving him all kinds of hell. Demanding to know where he'd been."

Griffon closed his eyes and dug his fingers into his sockets as if he could erase the memory—the happening—if he could only erase the picture in his mind. "The moment I lost my temper, everything unraveled. My anger tripped Sean's, and he'd always been a ferocious scrapper. He came at me with his fists balled and his voice just as loud and angry as mine, telling me I had no right to tell him what to do. That I wasn't his old man."

He rubbed the back of his neck and drew a deep, shaky breath. "And I lost it. Completely. If he thought he could jerk me around and worry me to death because I wasn't the old man, I was gonna show him I could damned well be just as mean. I doubled my fist and I hit him with all my power. I can still hear the pop of bone, see the blood gushing from his nose." The last words were a bare whisper.

Dear heaven. She, too, could imagine the ugly scene. But the devastation Griffon had felt, she didn't have to imagine. It was still in his face. She wanted to go to him. Put her arms around him. Comfort him. But he would close up if she did. And very well walk out on her. So she pushed on. "What did you do then?"

"I ran. One glance at my brother's blood pouring onto the floor, one glance at the betrayal in his face, and I ran. For hours. And then I walked for hours. By the time the sun was peeking over the horizon I knew I couldn't go back to that trailer. And I knew those kids couldn't take care of themselves. So I did the one thing we'd promised each other we'd never do. I called Social Services. Told them there were three kids under eighteen living in that trailer. That their mother was dead and their father beat them and they needed someone to take care of them. And then I went back to the trailer park and hid behind one of the neighbor's trailers until Social Services came and took them away."

They. Them. Her heart ached and her stomach rolled. "You didn't go with them?"

He shook his head. "I went to the street. I didn't want to go to some foster home. I knew decent people wouldn't want a monster like me living with them. And I sure as hell wasn't going back to that trailer."

"The street? How did you survive?"

Another ugly laugh. "Just like I did at home. Using my wits to find food and clothing and my fists to stay intact. Then when I turned eighteen I ran to the nearest army recruiter's office and signed up. I figured three squares a day, a roof over my head and a steady paycheck was a hell of a step up."

She sorted through all the information to come back to the sticking point. "Hitting your brother was an ugly mistake, Griffon. But that's all it was. A mistake."

He shook his head. "Being raised the way I was *I* should have been the last person to resort to violence. I hated it. I can't tell you how many times I held my brother or sisters after the old man had beaten them and swore I would never be like him. But the violence is in my blood. There's no getting away from it."

Realization streaked through her. "*This* is that blood nonsense you were spouting last night."

He narrowed his eyes on her. "It's not nonsense. Psychologists can spout all the crap they want about environment versus genealogy, but I can tell you violence is in the blood. The afflicted can try to control it. I learned techniques in the army to help keep it under wraps. But it never goes away. It's always there, waiting just under my tenuous shell of control to take hold of me, turn me into the monster I really am. That's why I stayed a soldier. The battlefield gives me a safe place to spend that violence.''

She stared at him, unable to speak. He believed he was a monster. She could see the absolute certainty in his eyes. Fear skidded up her spine. How was she ever going to make him see it wasn't so? How was she going to make him see he belonged in his daughter's life? In her life? That he wasn't a monster that belonged locked behind high fences and razor wire when he wasn't on the battlefield.

She turned a hand up in supplication. ''Griffon, what happened that night had nothing to do with blood and everything to do with the way you were raised. And your age. Don't you see, you were a fifteen-year-old boy with no parenting skills and fewer life skills. Lord, a lot of fifteen-year-old boys who'd been raised right might have smacked their brother in the nose that night. Not that I'm condoning it,'' she quickly amended. ''It's just that it was an honest mistake. A very honest mistake for a boy who'd been raised like you.''

He snorted. ''You're naive if you believe that.''

She shook her head. ''No, I'm not. This isn't about naivety, it's about fear. I'm not afraid you'll hurt anyone. And you are.'' Frustration made her voice sharp.

''Is that little dig supposed to challenge my manhood? You think you can embarrass me into being a father so I won't have to admit I'm afraid of something?" He huffed in disgust. "I *am* afraid. I know what it's like to have a man ten times my size stand over me with rage and fury contorting his face. I know what it's like to feel his fists beat me to a pulp. I won't put my own child through that. No way in hell."

"Of course you won't. And not because you'll isolate yourself. You won't because *you're not your father.*" Her voice was louder than it should have been. But she couldn't help it. She had to get through to him.

"I *am* my father. Believe me."

"You're not anything like your father. You're kind and gentle and...valiant." Why couldn't he see that?

He laughed that cold, hollow laugh again. "No, I'm not. Just ask any of the men I fight with. They'll tell you exactly what kind of man I am."

She gritted her teeth, her patience running out fast. She could drag his entire company in here and they would—one and all—tell him what a wonderful man he was. But he wouldn't believe them any more than he was willing to believe her.

But she would be damned if she'd give up. There had to be *something* she could say to make him see how wrongheaded he was. "You can't define yourself by what happens on the battlefield. Those men you fight are your enemies. They're killing your men and the people you're trying to protect. They're trying to kill *you,*" she stressed, her voice rising in frustration. "They deserve your wrath. But you would *never* hurt someone you loved, Griffon. *Never.* It isn't in you."

His lip curled in a frustrated snarl. "You don't know what you're talking about."

She leaped from the sofa and stalked over to him until they were toe-to-toe. "Of *course* I know. When I handed Perry off to you the other day, she was crying her head off—and you were strung tighter than a piano wire. But did you a hurt her? *No.* You took her down to the stream and built stone castles with her, for pity's sake. And when you found me hanging from your roof, you were *furious.* Did you hit me? Did you hurt me in any way? *No.* You kissed me. *Kissed* me."

Righteous anger boiled through, spiking her temper and raising her voice. "And right now you're so mad at me I'm surprised you're not spitting nails. But you're not. You're swallowing your anger and your bruised pride, and you're doing everything in your power to help me see that your baby will be better off without you. And you're doing it because you want to make sure your baby is safe. That isn't the kind of man who is ever going to hit his child, Griffon. Or anyone else."

"Give it up, Juliana. It isn't going to work." His words were a low, guttural growl—his expression just as dark, just as angry as she imagined hers was.

A loud, distressed wail erupted in the cabin. Startled, they both turned to Perry. She was sitting in the fireplace, staring at them, her expression startled, her cries uncertain and frightened.

Juliana's heart clenched. Perry didn't understand what was going on between her and Griffon. She'd never seen anyone fight before. Taking a hard rein on the emotions pounding through her, Juliana rushed over to her and scooped her up. "Shhh, baby it's okay."

Remorse filled Griffon's face. "It's not okay. This is exactly what I was talking about." He turned to the door.

"Wait, we're not done." She rushed across the room, grabbed hold of his sleeve and pulled him back around.

"Oh, we're done." His eyes were filled with the darkest shadows she'd ever seen. "I know you want to believe that I'm not my old man. But all you have to do is look at your daughter's face to know I'm right. Do you know how many times I heard my brother and sisters cry like that when my old man hurt them or frightened them? A million. And now I've done the same thing to my own child." He took a step toward the door.

She held on to his sleeve as if it were a lifeline, refusing to let him go. "This is not the same thing. True, in the future we'll have to be sure Perry isn't within earshot if we're going to have a heated discussion. But what just happened was *not* the same as what your father did to your family. You weren't being mean or nasty. You weren't trying to intimidate anyone. You didn't *hit* anyone, Griffon. I would be willing to bet that besides your brother, and instances of self-defense, you have *never* hit anyone.

"You're *not* a fifteen-year-old boy with no support and no tools to fight with anymore. You're a grown man who knows how to handle his problems in a civilized manner. A grown man with the gentlest, most giving heart I've ever known.''

She locked her gaze onto his, willing him to believe her, willing him to see the truth. ''You'll never be an abuser, Griffon. Can't you see that?''

He wanted to believe it. She could see the wishful longing in his eyes. But he didn't believe it. A lifetime of neglect, a lifetime of abuse, a lifetime of violence was keeping him from it. The demons were winning. Dear Lord, they were winning.

He pushed a stray strand of hair behind her ear and gave her a sad smile. ''You're fighting a losing battle, Juliana. If you give it some thought, you'll realize I'm right.'' Pulling free of her fingers, he headed for the door.

Pain tore at her heart. She wasn't going to be able to save this. He was going to walk out of their lives. And he wasn't ever going to walk back in. She shook her head. ''Too bad you won't stay, Griffon. You almost had me convinced.''

He paused halfway out the door and turned back to her.

''You almost convinced me that someone might want me just for myself. Not for my social status or my money or my power. But just for me.''

Pain flashed in his eyes. Pain and regret. But it didn't stop him. Without another word he turned on his heels and left, pulling the door closed behind him.

Chapter Fifteen

Griff sat in his office, staring out the window to the courtyard. The sun was shining, the sky was blue and the flowers bloomed big and bright. But he didn't give a damn about any of that. The only thing that mattered was the high whine of the jet's engine as it warmed up on the tarmac. Warmed up so it could take Juliana and Perry back home.

Every muscle in his body screamed at him to get out of his chair and race to the runway, stop the jet, pull Juliana out of it and into his arms. But he couldn't do that. He *couldn't*. Letting that plane take off, sending Juliana and Perry as far from him as he could was the right decision.

Even if it was tearing his heart out.

There was a sharp rap on his door. Then it swung open, and Rand Michaels strode in.

Griff turned from the window. He'd been waiting for the man all morning and he was glad he was finally here. Glad he finally had a distraction. And glad to see the soldier had returned from the field in one piece, if not totally undamaged.

Griff assessed Rand's condition in a glance. The man was battered and bruised. One eye was black, his lip was split and he leaned ever so slightly to one side, which indicated he probably had a few bruised if not broken ribs. But the man was walking. Which meant there was no damage that a little time and rest wouldn't heal.

Good, now they could get down to business. "What the hell happened out there?"

Rand lowered himself into the chair opposite Griff with a wince and a spate of curses. "What the hell *didn't* happen? The bust went sour, the weapons went missing and that smooth-talking bastard I was supposed to be working *with* ran out with the money." Rand ran a frustrated hand down his face. "Dammit, I knew I couldn't trust that weasel."

"Then why did you?" Griff regretted his sharp tone the minute the question was out of his mouth. Rand was a good man. His talent with languages and quick mind made him one hell of an undercover agent. And he was a trusted friend. Griff knew Rand had done everything in his power to make the mission run smoothly.

But Griff was feeling every bit as battered as Rand looked. And the sound of those damned engines pounded at his ears like concussion grenades, making his temper short.

"I didn't trust him." Anger vibrated in every one of Rand's words. "But there was only so much I could do to shape the mission. I wasn't in charge, remember? The government agency the bastard worked for was. I was just there to help. Or get duped, as it turned out."

"Well, if it's any consolation, they got duped, too. And they aren't any happier about it than you."

"Serves them right."

"Maybe it does. But they sure as hell don't see it that way. They're hopping mad. And you're under suspicion for helping the weasel get away."

Fury leaped into Rand's eyes. "Well, you can tell them they can take their suspicions and—"

Griff held his hand up. "I told them if they thought you were involved, they needed to reassess the situation. And that there would be plenty of time to discuss blame and culpability in the next few days. That right now you needed time to rest and heal." He canted his head toward Rand's midsection. "Any broken bones we need to worry about?"

"No. Bruised and sore as hell, but not broken."

"Good. Now go hit the sack. You look like hell."

A wry smile turned Rand's lips. "Thanks." He pushed up from the chair, but paused just before he went out the door, his expression dark. "I don't care if the agency that bastard worked for ever gets their damned money. But I want those weapons back before they kill anyone. And I want that low-life, pretty-boy Taylor."

Griff understood the feeling perfectly. He wanted to pound somebody, too. Unfortunately, he had no one other than himself to focus his anger on. In that respect Rand was a lucky man. Griff nodded. ''Fine. But first get some rest. Tomorrow will be soon enough to look for blood.''

With another nod Rand pulled the door closed behind him.

Griff stared at the closed portal. That boy was in big trouble. But Griff wasn't going to dwell on it now. He had problems of his own.

There was nothing to mute the sound of the engines now. Nothing to distract his aching heart. The high whine grated on his ears and lashed at his soul. Five minutes from now, maybe less, Juliana and Perry would be in the air, on their way back to Bjorli.

On their way away from him.

Frustration and anger pounded through him. Damn his cursed life. He couldn't remember a time when he hadn't had to fight for survival. Couldn't remember a day that wasn't a test of endurance. Would he survive his father's beatings? Would he survive this battlefield? Would he survive that one? And now the only two, truly good things he ever managed to bring into his life were leaving.

And he couldn't bring them back.

Damn it all to hell.

He pushed up from his chair and paced around the room like a caged tiger, the sound of the plane's engines driving him like a cruel captor's whip. And as the engines got louder, turning into a deafening roar, indicating the plane was hurtling down the runway, the whip lashed at him harder. Faster. A humongous roar filled the room as the plane jumped into the sky.

Slowly the sound faded into a low growl and finally receded until there was no sound at all...except his hard, labored breathing and the pounding of his heart and the weeping of his soul.

He closed his eyes and reminded himself that sending them home, sending them away from him, was the right thing to do. But it didn't make him feel any better. It didn't make the pain in his chest go away or the anger pounding at his temples stop. He clenched his hands into fists. He couldn't stay here one more minute. He needed a diversion. A bone-crunching diversion. He strode out of the office and headed for the gym.

The silent halls mocked him as he strode beneath their tall ceilings. Everywhere he looked he saw Juliana striding in her tight jeans and protest T-shirt. Or Perry crawling across the floor in one of her ruffly dresses.

He closed his eyes, trying to block out the memories, the loneliness that threatened to swallow him whole. But the darkness was no refuge. It engulfed him, trapped him, letting all the demons from his past rush at him like a stampeding army.

His father's image swam before him, his eyes bloodshot with alcohol, wild with fury. The old man's lips twisted into a contorted, savage sneer. His fists doubled up, ready to swing at Griff.

And the old man's vicious laughter echoed in Griff's head as clearly as it had twenty years ago, screaming at Griff that he'd never amount to anything. That he was stupid and worthless. That he'd never be anything but a trouble-making screw-up.

Griff snapped his eyes open with a start—cold sweat covering his skin.

He *had* amounted to something, dammit. He'd become a successful soldier and he'd built a damned impressive business out of it. Made a fortune at it. He'd bought a *mansion* with his earnings. A hell of a step up from the run-down, rat-infested trailer his old man had been able to afford.

The laughter and voice echoed through his head again. ''You won't find any more joy in those fancy halls than you found in my trailer, boy.''

Griff strode faster, trying to block the ugly words from his mind. But the voice was right. These halls might be fancy, but without the two people that could have turned them into a home, they held just as much despair as that hellish trailer had.

He thought desperately of the cabin—the laughter he'd shared there, the feeling of family and home that had filled him as he and Perry and Juliana had made that pie.

But the cabin wouldn't feel like that now. It wouldn't feel warm or homey with no one to laugh within its walls. It would be just as empty and lonely as this place. Griff laughed, the sound raw and hollow. He'd worked and fought and spilled his blood to create something more than the empty desolation he'd left behind twenty years ago. But in the end he had *nothing* but the cold, ugly legacy his father had left him.

The church's doors loomed before him. Slamming through them, he strode into the gym. Normally the place was busy this time of today. But today the only occupant was Talon. The lone soldier threw one rapid punch after the other at one of the sandbags.

Griff grimaced. His least favorite sparring partner. But today, with no one else in the gym, he'd settle. He strode into the cavernous room, grabbed two pairs of sparring gloves and headed toward Talon. "Hey Redhorse, up for a few rounds?"

Talon stepped away from the swinging bag and turned to him with a smile that held far too many teeth. "You got here quicker than I thought."

Griff tossed him a set of the gloves. "What's that supposed to mean?"

Talon easily caught them and pulled them on. "It means I heard the plane take off. I thought for sure you'd brood around for at least half an hour before making your way down here."

Griff shot him a deadly glare. "You want to spar or gossip?"

The smile got a little wider. "Spar."

They moved to the matts in the center of the room, raised their hands and began circling each other, each looking for an opening. Griff threw the first punch. He didn't care if he had an opening or not. He just wanted to hit something.

Talon easily blocked the wild punch and threw one of his own, landing it with stinging accuracy.

Griff's head slammed back. Pain exploded in his jaw, and lights danced in his eyes. Stepping out of range, he shook his head, forcing his vision to refocus.

Talon came after him, his eyes sharp as he looked for another opening. "You better get your head in the game, brother. Or you're going to walk out of here with a few less teeth in that thick head of yours.'' Talon feinted one direction, ducked in the other and threw another punch.

Griff danced to the left and blocked it before it connected with his ribs.

Talon circled, his fists up, his feet moving. ''Of course, I can understand why you might have trouble concentrating. That was a pretty lady you put on the plane. A nice lady. And the baby. She was a cutie, wasn't she?''

Despair slid through Griff, followed by a hot shot of anger. He didn't need this man telling him what he'd just sent away. He landed a solid blow to the man's gut. ''What's wrong with you, Redhorse? Normally we can't pull a word out of you, but today you can't seem to shut up.''

''Usually, I don't have anything to say.''

''You don't have anything to say today, either.'' Griff landed another solid punch.

Talon grunted and fell back, but his maddening smile never wavered. ''You're right, I'm worrying about nothing. She's a pretty a lady. Some man will snatch her up. Take care of her. Warm her bed.''

Griffon saw red, but he held his temper in check. He'd seen Talon at work on the sparring floor before. The man picked at his opponent with stinging jabs and painful punches until the other fighter lost his temper. Then the warrior settled into a hard, no-holds-barred, let's-see-if-we-can-kill-each-other fight. A fight that fed a dark need that Talon had, to punish himself. Today Talon wasn't using his fists to push

Griff's temper over the edge. He was using words. But he was after the same result.

And Griff wasn't going to play.

Talon wasn't his enemy. He was one of his men. A friend. The last thing he wanted to do was beat the man to a bloody pulp, even in his current mood.

Griff froze, sudden realization sinking into him like a well-aimed bayonet. He took a step back, dropped his hands, dropping his guard.

But Talon was unprepared for his sudden surrender and his next blow, a hard uppercut, connected with Griff's jaw, lifting him off the ground and sending him sailing.

Griff landed on his hands and knees, his jaw aching and his head spinning. But more from Juliana's words than the punch.

You can't define yourself by what happens on the battlefield. Those men you fight are your enemies. They're trying to kill you. They deserve your wrath. But you would never hurt someone you loved, Griffon. Never.

God help him, she was right.

There was a difference between fighting the enemy and hurting someone he cared for. A very definite difference. Although anger still exploded within him when he saw the strong abusing the weak, he would never use his power against Juliana or Perry.

Or anyone else who didn't deserve it.

Never.

Ever.

Taking a steadying breath, he sat back on his

haunches and dabbed at the blood dripping from his lip. He stared at the room around him with new eyes, the gym equipment, the high ceilings, the stained-glass windows filled with divine grace and brother-hood.

Somewhere along the line, somewhere between leaving that hellish trailer and this moment, he had ceased to be that angry, frustrated fifteen-year-old boy and shed his father's legacy of violence. He'd ceased to be a man who fought on the battlefields to vent his rage and he'd become a man who fought so a few more people could have a little of the peace he'd never known.

A slow smile curved his lips. He had to wonder if that change hadn't begun two years ago when the most beautiful woman in the world had offered him a cup of hot cocoa and a piece of her heart.

"Are you going to get up or are we done for the day?" Talon's voice pulled him out his musing.

Pushing himself to his feet, Griff headed for the door. "We're done."

"Are you sure?" Talon called after him. "I'll be happy to give you a free shot. I owe you one for that last blow. I didn't catch you lowering your guard in time."

Griff glanced over his shoulder. "One of these days we'll have to discuss why you think it's necessary to punish yourself this way, Redhorse."

Talon's eyes narrowed to deadly black slits.

Griff laughed. "Don't worry. Not today. Today I have a plane to turn around."

* * *

Juliana sat in the plane, Perry on her lap, the whine of the engines in her ears.

And her heart breaking into a million tiny pieces.

She hugged Perry tight and buried her nose in her soft, silky hair. "It looks like it's just you and me, sweetie pie. Just you and me." The words died away in a shaky whisper.

She'd hoped all day yesterday and all of this morning, right up until the moment the plane actually left the ground, that Griffon would come to her, tell her he'd changed his mind, tell her he'd been wrong, that they had a chance together.

She'd hoped he would come to her and tell her he loved her.

But he hadn't.

Because like all the men who'd gone before him, he didn't love her. At least not enough. If he did, he would have fought for her. He would have fought to stay with them. He would have…

She stopped, her mind grinding to a wavering, unsteady halt.

Wait a minute. All the other men in her life had clung to her like she was their lifeline. Even after she dumped them and sent them on their way they'd come back, trying to get in her good graces again, trying to hold on to their path to fortune and power. Even Brandon, the slime-bucket, had come around the next morning with sweet words and some convoluted excuse for his toast the night before. And she'd not only told him in no uncertain terms to get lost that night, she'd dumped the entire bottle of champagne on his head to make sure he'd gotten the point.

But Griffon wasn't clinging.

He was sending her away.

So he wouldn't hurt her.

He *was* fighting for her. In a stupid, crazy, wrong-headed manner, yes. But still...he was fighting for her. *Her.* Not her position or her power.

Her.

Her heart tripped and sputtered and then surged with jubilation.

He loved her.

Tears splashed onto her cheeks.

He loved her.

And she loved him.

So what was she doing on this plane?

She unbuckled her seat belt and settled Perry on her hip. "Come on, sweetie pie." She headed for the front of the plane.

Halfway to the cockpit, her guard stepped in front of her. "Is there something I can get for you, Ms. Bondevik?"

"I need to talk to the pilot."

"He's flying the plane, ma'am."

She gave him a disparaging look. "Please don't tell me we have a pilot who can't manage a simple conversation and flying his plane at the same time. My father would be most displeased to think such an incompetent man was flying his daughter."

The soldier grimaced. "No, ma'am. He can talk and fly at the same time."

"Then show me to the cockpit, soldier."

With another grimace he headed down the aisle. "This way, ma'am."

The pilot turned to them the minute they entered the cabin.

She gave the man an easy smile. "Good morning, Captain. I need you to turn this plane around and take us back to the compound."

Surprise flashed in the man's eyes. "Ma'am, I can't just—"

The radio squawked.

"Excuse me." He listened intently to his head phones, said something she couldn't hear into the microphone and then turned his attention back to her. "No problem, ma'am. I'll turn the plane around as you requested, immediately."

Juliana thought that was a quick change of attitude, but since it was in her favor she wasn't going to argue. "Good. And will you please have one of the men bring my bag back to the rest room." There was something in there she needed.

"I can do that, ma'am. But I can't land until you're back in your seat and buckled in."

"Then you might have to circle for a few minutes, Captain."

Chapter Sixteen

Juliana smoothed the tight, bright material over her hip. She'd spent the last twenty minutes in the plane's cramped bathroom dressing for effect. Major effect.

The last dress she'd worn for Griffon had been demure. This one was anything but. It was a class-A, hey-big-boy, knuckle biter. The electric-blue spandex made her eyes pop and her curves stand out like flashing neon. The neckline plunged far beyond the teasing range, and the hemline ended far above the risky range.

She dropped a quick kiss on Perry's head as she waited for the plane's doors to open. "Think your daddy will like it, sweetie pie?"

Lord, she needed him to like it. More than like it. She needed to dazzle him—stun him. At least long enough that she could make her case before he tried to shove her on the plane and send her back to Bjorli. Not that she couldn't, or wouldn't, just get on a plane and head right back here if he did. But she would rather not have to. She'd spent enough time away from him in the past two years. She didn't want to lose another minute. And she hoped the sexy little number she never could have imagined herself wearing before would help her win her case.

She held her breath and prepared for battle as the soldier opened the plane's door to allow her to disembark. And then she was walking down the stairs, looking for her target.

He stood next to a Jeep parked at the edge of the runway

Tall and handsome and oh, so dear.

Heart racing and palms sweating, she strode steadily toward him.

His gaze locked on her like a couple of lasers, dark green edging toward midnight as he took in every detail, every curve, every inch of exposed skin.

Desire and pleasure shot through her. She'd dazzled him. Now all she had to do was make him understand she didn't intend to go anywhere. She pulled her gaze from his eyes, taking in the rest of his dear face. And that's when she saw the split lip and the discoloration at his jaw. What on earth? She rushed forward, reaching for his face. "What happened? Are you all right?"

He pulled back just far enough to keep her from touching the split lip. "I'm fine."

"No, you're not. You're bleeding.

He touched a finger to the red angry spot. "It's nothing. I just bit it."

Yeah, right. She took a step forward, touched his chin and tipped his head to the side, exposing a good-size, still-blackening injury. "With a little help."

A smile quirked his lips. "With a little help."

She narrowed her eyes on him. "Whose help?" She'd have a serious talk with that soldier.

His lips twitched again. "With that look in your eye I think I'd best keep that private." He tipped his head toward her dress. "Is that for me?"

Heat stole into her cheeks, but she wasn't backing down now. She raised her chin. "Yes."

His eyes sparkled. "Beautiful."

She drew a deep breath and plunged ahead. "I'm glad you like it. It was a diversion. I thought it might keep you quiet long enough for me to tell you I'm not going back to Bjorli. You can stick me on your plane if you want, but I'll just come back. I'll buy a little bit of land outside your compound and build a house on it if I have to. But I'm going to stay here until you figure out that we belong together."

He raised a brow, that half smile never leaving his lips. "Is that right?"

She lifted her chin another notch and went for broke. "I love you Griffon. I love the way you think you have to save the world. And the way your eyes darken when you look at me like you did just now. And I love your gentleness." She locked her gaze to his, waiting for him to object. When he didn't, she went on. "And I think you love me. I know you want to deny it. I know it might be a while before you can say it to me, before you can admit it to yourself even, but—''

''I love you.''

She froze. Her heart pounding like a humming-bird's wings. ''Excuse me?''

He chuckled softly, his hand reaching out to tuck a strand of hair behind her ear. ''I love you. And I have no intention of putting you back on that plane. Or letting you camp outside the compound, either, for that matter.''

She swallowed hard and licked her lips. ''Did you just say you loved me? And that I don't have to get back on the plane?''

He nodded, his smile full-blown now.

Her heart pounded with confusion and fear and giddy hope. ''What are you saying?'' The words were a bare whisper.

''I'm saying, I figured it out. It took a while.'' He smiled wryly. ''And a few good punches, but I finally realized you were right. I'm not that fifteen-year-old boy anymore. I'll never hurt you. Or Perry. But if you say you'll marry me I will love you and treasure you and cherish you until the day I die.'' He cupped Perry's head, his big hand gently stroking the baby's hair. ''Both of you.''

Her heart stopped, her world spun. Had he just said what she thought he had? Had he just proposed to her? She stood stunned.

''Juliana? Will you marry me? I know it's sudd—''

He had proposed to her! She threw her free arm around him, her heart exploding with happiness. ''Yes. I'll marry you.''

He lowered his lips to hers for a quick hard kiss and then he hugged them both tight. "God, how could I ever have thought of letting either of you go?"

She snuggled closer, drinking in the feel of him. His strength. His warmth. His love. She could stay right here, the three of them locked in this embrace, forever. And speaking of the three of them. There was something important she had to do.

She pulled back slightly. "Griffon Tyner, I'd like to introduce you to your daughter...Persephone Lockland, my mother's maiden name," she explained, "Bondevik. Soon to be, Persephone Lockland Tyner."

A smile bright enough to light the darkest of nights turned his lips. Tears sparkled in his eyes. "How wonderful to meet you, beautiful Persephone." He turned to Juliana, smiling. "The goddess of spring. And renewal. I like it."

She nodded, fighting her own tears of happiness. "It's rather appropriate don't you think?"

He gave Juliana another heated kiss. "Absolutely." Taking hold of her hand he pulled them toward the Jeep. "Come on, let's take her home."

Juliana followed him in a contented daze for a few steps, but then a tiny bit of reality reared its head and she pulled to a halt. "Griffon, wait. Where is home going to be?"

He turned back to her with a befuddled look, and then a rueful, almost boyish smile curved his lips. "I don't know. This hit me kind of sudden. I haven't had time to think about the details. I guess I thought we'd live in the mansion because my operation is here. But I could move Freedom Rings to Bjorli if it's important to you."

She shook her head. "I don't want to live in Bjorli. I want to spend the rest of my life as a normal citizen, not the chancellor's daughter." She cupped his jaw, drinking in his rugged, bruised features. "As Mrs. Tyner. But I don't want to live in your mansion, I want Perry to grow up like a normal little girl, in a normal little house."

He smiled, a gentle smile of indulgence and inner peace. "I know a little cabin by a stream. It's small now, but we could add on. Put in electricity. Plumbing."

Joy burst through her. Tears stung her eyes.

A mother, a father, a tiny house, a tinier child...

And love.

"A dream come true." She captured his lips with hers.

* * * * *

ANN MAJOR
CHRISTINE RIMMER
BEVERLY BARTON

cordially invite you to attend the year's most exclusive party at the **LONE STAR COUNTRY CLUB!**

Meet three very different young women who'll discover that wishes *can* come true!

LONE STAR
COUNTRY CLUB:
The Debutantes

Lone Star Country Club: Where Texas society reigns supreme—and appearances are *everything*.

Available in May at your favorite retail outlet, only from Silhouette.

Award-winning author
SHARON DE VITA
brings her special brand of romance to

SPECIAL EDITION™
and

SILHOUETTE *Romance*™

in her new cross-line miniseries

SADDLE FALLS

This small Western town was rocked by scandal when the youngest son of the prominent Ryan family was kidnapped. Watch as clues about the mysterious disappearance are unveiled—and meet the sexy Ryan brothers...along with the women destined to lasso their hearts.

Don't miss:

WITH FAMILY IN MIND
February 2002, Silhouette Special Edition #1450

ANYTHING FOR HER FAMILY
March 2002, Silhouette Romance #1580

A FAMILY TO BE
April 2002, Silhouette Romance #1586

A FAMILY TO COME HOME TO
May 2002, Silhouette Special Edition #1468

Available at your favorite retail outlet.

Silhouette®
Where love comes alive™

Visit Silhouette at www.eHarlequin.com   SSERSFR

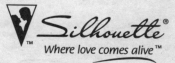